IT WAS ALWAYS YOU

S.L. STERLING

Dedication

Dedicated to my husband.
Thank you for always believing in me.

Prologue

I sat on the couch looking out the front window at the dark clouds rolling in. I heard thunder in the distance, and rain pounded on the glass.

"You need to decide, Tatum. I need to let them know in two days, or else this opportunity will be gone. I want you to move with me." Parker placed his hand under my chin, lifting my head so he could look into my eyes. "Please don't let this be the end of us. We are great together."

I swallowed hard. He had received an offer from the Emerald Bay Police Department. It was only a short eight-hour drive away, and he had to decide in forty-eight hours. I looked away from his crystal-blue eyes—eyes that would make any woman weak in the knees. "I'm not sure I can, Parker. I just got the job at that magazine. It won't look good if I change my mind and tell them I'm leaving. I'd also have a hard time leaving Elliott so soon after us losing Mom and Dad. I'm all he has now."

Stroking my hand as he held it in his, he placed his arm around me and pulled me into his muscular chest. I tried hard to hide the tears, but they escaped anyway.

"I know everything in your life has changed, and quick at that. I don't want you to feel as if I'm leaving you as well because that's not what I'm doing. If you're unsure about moving right away, how about we try a long-distance relationship? I'll go find us a place, get through the training and get on my feet, and then you can move down with me? It will give you time to put out resumes in the area. In the meantime, you can get experience working here, possibly get a referral." He wiped the tears from my face. I had always loved the feel of his warm, strong hand on my cheek. "Please, love, don't cry."

I thought about what he had suggested. The option sounded good, but something in my gut told me it wouldn't work. I wasn't sure if it was the fear of another major change in my life that was causing me to feel sick, or the fear of losing him. I was also afraid that in the time we would be apart that he would meet someone else. We would be looking at six months at least before we would be together, and a lot could happen in six months. "I know you have been through a lot of shit in the past year, and a lot of adjustments. Please don't shut me out. Talk to me, tell me what you're thinking." I could see his hopes disintegrating the longer I remained silent.

"What if it doesn't work out? I mean, it is long distance. It's not like we can be with one another every weekend. We'd be lucky to see one another once or twice out of the six months. Neither one of us can afford to fly or drive back and forth."

"No, you're right. But once my training is over in six weeks, I'll have blocks of time off and will be able to drive back here and stay with you."

"But I can't guarantee I'll have those days off and won't have work in the evening to do, so you'll be sitting here watching me."

Parker leaned forward and placed his head in his hands. "I would rather sit here watching you than not have you in my life."

"Parker, I am serious."

"So am I. It's only six months."

"I don't know, Parker." I looked up into his eyes and couldn't stop more tears from falling from my own.

"So then, what you're saying is this may be it for us?" I could hardly hear the words he muttered as he stood up.

"No, Parker, that's not what I am saying. I'm trying to be realistic."

I watched Parker walk toward the door. I didn't know what I was saying. A big part of me didn't want to be without him, even for a short period of time. I knew we could work through pretty much anything. The other part of me knew letting him go to concentrate on his new career was the right thing to do. The last thing he needed was to be worrying about me. I tried to take a deep breath, but felt choked.

"Doesn't sound like it. I've worked too hard to give up on this opportunity, Tatum. You seem to be making excuses. Elliott will be applying to the same force I am, and once he gets his call, he'll move away too. You're using work as a crutch to fight what you want because you're afraid."

Everything he was saying was true. I was afraid of another change, and it was killing me inside.

"I'm sorry, Tatum, but I have to go, and I'm sorry if you are not okay with it. I guess if this is it for us, then so be it."

Parker stopped and turned before he walked out the door and gave me a look I wished I could wash from my memory forever. "This"—he waved his finger between us —"is breaking my heart."

I stood to go to him. I wanted him to wrap me in his strong arms. And feel that embrace that, over the last couple years had healed the worst pain.

"I've got to go."

Tears poured down my cheeks, and my body shook. I went to the window and watched him walk down the front walkway, his head held low, and like that, he walked out of my life. I had never thought I would feel the pain of losing someone again so soon after Mom and Dad died. I especially never thought it would be Parker.

That night, Parker asked Elliott to drive him to the airport. Elliott told me that they were going to remain friends, even though we had broken up. I hoped they always would. After all, they had been friends before we started dating, and he was a good influence for my brother.

I was lying in bed when my phone rang. Parker's picture populated my screen. I knew I had made a huge mistake by not going with him or at least trying to make it work. I was too overwhelmed to deal with it right then, so I let the call go to voice mail. I curled up into the fetal position on my bed and cried. The last time I had laid this way, Parker had held me while I cried, not once letting me go throughout the night. How I longed to feel him behind me.

After an hour of tears, I played the message he had left. "I'm sorry that we ended things the way we did and without a true good-bye. I know in my heart that one day, we will find our way back to one another. I hope it doesn't take too long, but it will be what it will be. If you need me for anything, anything at all, please call or text me. I wish you luck with everything and want you to know that I love you."

My vision grew cloudy with tears, and my chest hurt. I couldn't help myself. Without hesitation, I dialed his number. I wanted to tell him I had made a mistake and would be on the next flight out, but it went straight to voice mail.

I wiped the tears from my cheeks and hung up my phone in time for the front door to open and Elliott to walk in. He gave my shoulders a squeeze as he walked by the couch. "How about we watch a movie?"

Chapter One

Tatum - 8 Years Later

I THREW MY PURSE ON THE COUCH AND HUNG MY JACKET on the back of the chair. Removing my shoes, I let my feet sink into the plush carpet. It had been a long week, and I was glad the day had come to an end. I had left work early tonight. It was our one-year anniversary, and Dean was taking me to a steak house for dinner, and then to a hotel for the night. Wanting to be ready when he picked me up, I turned the radio to the hits station and headed to the bathroom.

I stepped out of the shower and wrapped a towel around me then towel dried my hair and wiped the fog off the mirror. Looking at my reflection, my stomach did a little flip as soon as the thought of Dean entered my mind.

"I need to cancel our date again. I am sorry, but they need me to work late tonight on the case."

Being a partner in the law firm was important to Dean, but I had a sinking feeling that the last few times he had canceled on me wasn't because of work. Our relationship hadn't been the greatest lately. He seemed withdrawn, short-tempered, and demanding. He was always on his phone messaging people.

I went to the kitchen and poured myself a glass of wine. I took a sip, letting the cool liquid slide down my throat while checking for messages on my phone. Swiping at the screen, I saw a message from Dean.

DEAN: WILL BE ABOUT AN HOUR LATE, COURT WENT OVERTIME, AND I DON'T WANT TO HEAR IT.

"Of course it did," I mumbled. Throwing my phone down on the counter, I headed back to my bedroom with my wine.

Going to my closet, I started sorting through my dresses, finally deciding on my favorite little black cocktail dress. It fit me in all the right places, and I wanted to look good for Dean. He was always complaining that I never looked good enough. I had finished my makeup when my phone rang, my stomach doing another flip as I answered.

"Did that douche cancel on you yet?" Elliott's voice poured over the phone. He had a major dislike for Dean and didn't have any problem showing it.

I smiled into the phone. I missed him something terrible. Three years ago, he moved to pursue his dreams of becoming a cop. He had been sent to the undercover unit six months ago and was just about to complete his training. "Hey, Elliott. No, he hasn't canceled, but he will be late. I appreciate you checking in on me with such high hopes," I giggled.

"Well, text me if he does, and the next time I'm in town, I'll come and kick his ass. I can't have someone treat my little sister that way." He laughed into the phone.

All joking aside, I knew he was serious.

I gave a small smile. Elliott had always looked after me. "How are things, Elliott? How is work going?"

"Going great! I'm loving it. It has been challenging, that's for sure. Hey, I got something for you. I bet you'll never guess who my training officer is for this new department."

"How would I even begin to guess who your trainer is, Elliott?" I took another sip of my wine.

"It's Parker." In an instant, it was as if all the air had been sucked out of the room. "Tatum, did you hear me?"

I swallowed hard; thanking God Elliott couldn't see my reaction. I downed the rest of my wine. My mind was running in all different directions. I wondered what he looked like now. Was he married with kids? Why had I never bothered to get in touch with him? I took a deep breath, trying to silence my mind. "Well, at least I know you're in good hands. How is he?"

"He's doing well. I stayed with him after I got hired on the unit, my apartment was under renovation. It's been easier having someone here that I know, which reminds me, when are you coming down to visit me?"

"I have time off at the end of the month. I should be able to come down then. Dean will be away." I added more wine to my glass, having a hard time believing I had let that slip out.

"Dean will be away? I don't understand why that would matter. You're coming to visit your brother."

Taking notice of the time on the clock, I needed to get going and finish getting ready. "Elliott, I have to go. Dean should be here shortly."

"Tatum, I'd like an answer before we get off the phone."

"I mean, I won't have other engagements on my week off is all." Truth was, Dean didn't like Elliott either, and he didn't want me to see him anymore. We had had some major arguments the last few times Elliott had come back home. The last argument ended with me being forbidden to see my brother.

"Okay..." He was hesitant. "Remember, I'm always here if you need me to come up and kick him around. Just say the word."

After we said our good-byes, I started working on my hair, but my mind kept wandering to Parker. I hadn't thought of him since I met Dean. I always wondered what would have happened if I had moved with him.

Picking up my cell phone, I swiped to the contacts screen and pulled Parker's information up.

His contact picture opened, and I stared into that face, those eyes that still made my panties damp. If I thought hard enough, I could still feel his arms around me. My body pressed into his hard, well-defined chest. I could imagine those sexy, full lips kissing my lips and my neck, and his strong hands touching my body. Hands I still wished had explored every part of my body.

I clicked the text icon next to his name and typed hello then stared at the blinking cursor, trying to get up the courage to hit send, but hit delete instead. Who was I kidding? He wouldn't want to hear from me.

I wondered what his wife looked like, how cute his kids would be. "She is lucky to have you," I whispered to his photo.

I shut the phone off and concentrated on fixing my hair. Without warning, a feeling of pure regret poured over me. I would regret that breakup for the rest of my life.

"DID YOU ENJOY DINNER?" DEAN QUESTIONED AS HE pulled up to the hotel's valet parking and put the car in park.

"Yes, it was amazing. I would have enjoyed it more had you put your phone on silent and paid attention to us. It kept going off. What could be that important at eight o'clock on a Friday night?" The valet opened the door for me, and I climbed out of the car then grabbed my small bag from the back seat.

"What I was needed for doesn't concern you, now does it? I will make sure everything is wrapped up once we are in the room. It should only take me about forty-five minutes, and then you will have my undivided attention. I hope that meets your approval." Glaring at me, Dean ripped the bag from my hand, and without waiting for me, walked into the hotel.

"I'm sorry. I guess I've missed you these past few weeks. I wanted to have you all to myself tonight. You are leaving Sunday for a week," I whispered while standing in line waiting to check in.

Dean gave out a huff and stood with his body turned away from me, his face in his phone. He was responding to one email or text after another. Once again, I felt ignored as I had for the past few months.

"Give me some time when we get upstairs to take care of what I need to get finished, and then you'll have me all to yourself."

"I'll be over there." I moved to the nearest lounge, sat down and checked my phone. It was as if he didn't even hear me. I could feel tears threatening to fall. His short temper was making me feel as if he didn't want to be with me. Was there something so wrong with wanting to spend time with the person you love? I checked my email. When I unlocked my phone, the picture of Parker greeted me.

"What are you looking at?" I heard a rough voice demand, and I saw a hand reach out for my phone.

I shoved the phone into my jacket pocket before he could grab it from me. "Nothing, reading an email from work," I lied.

"Let's go," he demanded.

As soon as we arrived at our suite, Dean shut himself in the bedroom. I sent Elliott a quick message to let him know all was okay and that I would call him tomorrow. Not knowing how long Dean would be, I took my phone and headed into the bathroom. I turned the water on and filled up the Jacuzzi, disrobed, and climbed in. Lying back, I let the water cover my body and the heat soak on in, easing the stress and tension I was feeling.

Dean knocked on the door before opening it and brought in a glass of white wine. "I had room service bring up a bottle." He handed me the glass and sat on the edge of the tub. "Listen, one of the guys from the office is bringing over a couple documents I have to get signed tonight, so I am going to head down and meet him in the lobby. I shouldn't be too long."

Sighing, I took a sip and relaxed back in the water. "Whatever. Close the door please." I had nothing more to say. I could see that work would always come first, and I would always, no matter what, be on the back burner.

Dean glared into my eyes but said nothing. With the attitude I had been giving him, I knew I was pushing my luck. He stood and walked to the door, pulling it shut behind him. When the main door slammed shut, I started to cry. This was not how I pictured the evening going, never mind this relationship.

I stayed in the tub until I finished my wine, and with my chest aching and my eyes puffy and sore, I got out and dried off. Wrapping myself in one of the plush robes that hung on the back of the bathroom door, I went into the other room. Taking the spare blanket from the closet and a pillow from the bed, I poured myself another glass of wine, curled up on the couch, and found a movie on TV. *I figured*

I may as well enjoy part of the night. Dean was still downstairs, and it was probably for the best.

I awoke to sunlight beaming into my eyes. The last time I checked the clock, it was midnight. I guessed Dean's quick document signing turned into drinks and food.

I looked around the room. The TV was still on, and the door to the bedroom was open. I got up and walked over to the door to see if Dean was still in bed, but he wasn't. In fact, the bed hadn't even been slept in.

I walked over to the bathroom and peeked in; he wasn't in there either. Had he even returned to the room last night? I got dressed and went in search of Dean.

I took the elevator down to the lobby. When it stopped, I stepped out but came to an abrupt halt at what I saw. There, sitting on a couch in the center of the lobby, was Dean holding some blonde woman in his lap. I didn't know what to do. I didn't want him to see me, so I hid around the corner, peeking around so I could watch.

He was still wearing the clothes he had worn to dinner last night. The only thing missing was his tie and suit jacket. The woman kissed him deeply, and then rose from his lap. Dean stood and pulled her into him and kissed her again.

The lump in my throat made it hard for me to swallow. I watched as he whispered into her ear, and she giggled and kissed him again. She grabbed a small suitcase and walked out of the lobby. Dean watched until she was out of sight then grabbed a paper off the table in front of him and headed toward another set of elevators across the lobby.

I needed air... I could feel myself starting to panic. The

lobby began to spin, so I sat down in the chair nearest to me to catch my breath. I didn't want to face him. I didn't want to talk to him. I wanted to grab a cab and go home, but I had left everything upstairs.

When I didn't feel like I would be sick anymore, I made my way up to the room. I stood in the elevator trying to stop the deep, internal shake I could feel running through my body.

The elevator stopped on our floor, and the door opened. I took a deep breath before stepping into the hall and walking toward the room. I had a feeling something was going on with him, but I never thought it would be something like this.

With my hand shaking, I placed my key card into the lock and opened the door. Dean sat with his feet up on the coffee table, relaxing on the couch, reading the newspaper.

"Morning, sweetheart," Dean said, dropping the paper.

I said nothing. What on earth was there to say? I walked over and started packing my stuff.

"Sorry I didn't wake you when I returned last night. You were in bed and out like a light. You were still asleep when I went down to have breakfast and get a paper."

Every word he spoke was drilling another nail into my body.

"I thought we could go grab lunch and take a walk by the marina before I drop you at home. Sound good?" He came up behind me and wrapped his arms around me, hugging me from behind.

I shrugged myself out of his embrace and stuffed my pajamas into my bag. "Save it, Dean! I saw you!"

"You saw me?" he asked, rather surprised. "What is that supposed to mean?" he questioned.

"I saw you in the lobby a half hour ago." Turning around, I looked at him. "With her! You never came back here last night. You spent the night with her on our anniversary," I choked out. I marched into the bathroom to grab my toiletries.

"Honey, I don't know what you are talking about. I went downstairs last night to meet with a colleague to sign paperwork. We got to discussing business. It was almost two when I returned. I didn't want to wake you. I mean, I wanted to, but I thought you needed your sleep."

"Why are you lying? I saw you with a woman in your lap this morning dressed in a dark suit. She had blonde hair, and you were kissing her. You looked at her the way you used to look at me. I watched you kiss her good-bye, and then you grabbed the paper and headed toward the elevators. I saw it all, Dean. It definitely wasn't business. The bed hasn't even been slept in. I slept on the couch."

The tears gathered in the corners of my eyes. I didn't want to cry in front of him, but it was inevitable. "You must have pretty big balls, you know that? You bring me here on our anniversary, and while I sit here waiting like a fool, you go off and fuck another woman in the same hotel. You could have left me at home or broken up with me. How long has this been going on?"

His jaw clenched, and his hands balled into fists. "A while now, but I didn't expect..." He stopped mid-sentence to look at my face; it was streaked with tears.

"You didn't expect what? To be caught? I didn't expect

that I would spend the night alone with a bottle of wine. But I certainly didn't expect to find you with that whore on your lap!"

Dean towered over me and delivered a sharp slap across my face that took my breath away. "I've had enough of your fucking mouth," he snarled.

I stood there for a few moments, afraid at first to move. Once the shock wore off, I grabbed my purse and bag off the bed and ran over to the door.

He came at me, grabbing my shoulder. "Tatum, please. I'm sorry. I didn't mean for that to happen. Please don't end things like this. You're my girl. It was a mistake. I'll end it with her."

I pulled my shoulder away and opened the door. I turned to face him and tried to hide the pain he had inflicted on me. "You have ended it, and as for me being your girl, it is too late for that now," I whispered and shut the door behind me.

Chapter Two

Tatum

IT WAS ALMOST ONE O'CLOCK IN THE AFTERNOON ON Sunday, and the blinds were still drawn. I didn't want to have to face the cheeriness of the sunlight. I had spent the rest of the weekend in bed, resting my aching body against a pile of pillows. It hurt to breathe, and my eyes were dry and irritated from crying. I was sure the ache in my chest wasn't going to go away. My stomach gave the occasional rumble, crying out for food. Lying there, I realized I hadn't eaten since dinner on Friday night. After my stomach screamed out another round of hunger pains, I decided to get up and go see what I could shove in my face.

I headed to the kitchen to see what I could find. There wasn't much, considering I hadn't been shopping for a week, and the cupboards and fridge reflected that. I grabbed the phone and ordered in a large pizza. I put the phone down on the counter and caught a glimpse of myself in the hallway mirror. My eyes were dark and puffy, my hair was a tangled mess, and I looked like shit. Flopping down on the couch, I let out a deep sigh, grabbed the remote, and turned the TV on to the Food Network while I waited for my pizza.

An hour later, I lay on the couch, three-quarters of the pizza devoured, while watching some Italian broad cook pasta. My cell phone started vibrating, so I grabbed it off the table. There were three missed texts and two phone messages, all from Elliott. I listened to his messages first and could hear the concern in his voice. He always called when I didn't respond to his texts. I flipped through his texts. The last one threatened that if I didn't respond in the next twelve hours, he would be on the next plane. I shook my head. That was Elliott, always concerned about me.

I dialed his number, curled back up on the couch under a blanket, and waited for him to answer. "It's about fucking time, Tatum. You okay?" Hearing the panic in his voice made me realize how much he cared.

"Hey." I sniffled. "I'm okay."

"What is wrong? You don't sound okay." The line went silent. "What has that bastard done?"

I started to cry. "I caught him with another woman"

"When?"

"Friday night. All through dinner his phone kept going off with messages. I was upset and voiced my concern over it. He got his back up. He told me it was none of my business, but he had some work that needed to be taken care of. A while later, he said he was going to meet someone in the lobby to sign some paperwork. He left and I fell asleep. I woke to an empty room, and figuring he went for breakfast, I headed to the hotel restaurant. When I stepped out of the elevator, that is where I saw them, together, kissing in the lobby."

"Are you fucking serious?"

"Yes, I am. He spent the night in her hotel room."

"I knew there was something about that guy I didn't like. Do you need me to come up there?"

I could tell by his voice that Elliott was pissed, and I decided at that moment maybe Elliott didn't need to know about Dean slapping me. I didn't need to add any more fuel to the fire.

"No, Elliott, it's fine. I confronted him about it; he didn't deny it. I left him in the hotel yesterday morning, and I haven't heard anything from him." I grabbed some tissues to wipe the tears away.

"I can take some time off, Tatum. I'll tell work that there was an emergency with you, and I'll come home. I don't like the thought of you being alone right now."

"It's okay, Elliott. I go back to work tomorrow anyway, and Dean is out of town. Jen is here, too, so you don't need to worry."

"I need to do something, Tatum. Listen, if you won't let me come home, then you best promise me that you will come down here for a week or two. I can show you around, take you to the beach, hang out and watch movies like we used to or whatever else you want to do."

"I'm keeping my plans set for the end of the month. I can't take time off before then; we are pretty busy."

Elliott and I stayed on the phone for a few more hours. He told me all about his training and kept trying to cheer me up. I was so grateful to have a brother like him. When we finally hung up, I went to jump in the shower before bed. It was one in the morning before I crawled into bed, and I was exhausted. Monday morning would come early.

Chapter Three

Parker

I WALKED OUT OF THE STATION AND GOT INTO MY TRUCK. It had been a long shift, and Elliott hadn't made it go by any faster. Why did he have to bring up Tatum? It had been eight years, but they hadn't been easy. Truth was, I still missed her, and it hurt like hell. Sure, the hurt of her deciding to not move with me had diminished, but the hurt of wanting her was still there. Then he dropped it on me that she was going to visit, which meant I would see her. Was he warning me? Elliott and I spent all kinds of time together now that we were partners, so maybe this was a warning.

I started my truck and turned on the radio. What Hurts the Most by Rascal Flatts started playing which brought on even more memories of Tatum. This was her favorite song when we were in college, and I could never turn the station when it was on.

Why was I torturing myself? It wasn't as if I hadn't tortured myself every day for the last eight years. It was always over the fact I hadn't fought hard enough when she decided she couldn't move with me. God, I missed her.

The guys were back at the dorm waiting for me to study. I should have been in and out of the library in five minutes. After all, they had sent me in for a book I already had on hold. That was the first time I saw her.

I had been watching her for the past hour. I stood behind her, checking out her tight ass in her black yoga pants. She was waiting in line, waiting to check out a book she must have needed for one of her classes. The smell of her perfume invaded my senses. Between her ass and the smell of coconut, it was enough to make my dick twitch in my pants.

It was her turn at the counter. She handed the librarian the books and dug into her purse to get her library card. I watched as she fumbled through her bag and then did another check. "I swear I have my card." She was frantically searching now. "Can you look me up by name?" she asked.

"I'm afraid not. I must have your card," the librarian stated.

"I had it, I'm sure of it." Checking the floor around her, she went back to searching her bag. "I have a project to finish. Please, can't you help me out? I have my student card."

"I told you, I'm afraid not. No card, no books."

This woman had looked me up so many times by name. It pissed me off that she was giving her a hard time.

"Excuse me," I interjected, "I couldn't help but overhear. Did you lose your card?"

"I'm afraid I have." She looked up at me with the most beautiful light-hazel eyes—eyes you could get lost in.

I studied her face and watched as her full lips rounded into a soft smile. I'd love to know what those felt like against mine.

"I can help you out." I handed the librarian my card, not taking my eyes off hers. "Go ahead, check these books out on my account, and this one," I said, handing the librarian my book.

She looked at me, shrugged, checked out the books, and passed them to me.

"Thank you for that. If I didn't get those books, I wouldn't be able to finish my project." She smiled, her eyes traveling from my eyes to my lips. She took the books from me and tucked them into her bag.

"I'm Parker," I said, holding my hand out to her. "Glad I was able to help you out."

"Tatum." I watched her eyes scan my body as she slipped her soft hand into mine. Opening the door, a blast of cold hit us as we stepped out into the falling snow. "Well, again, thank you. I better get back to my dorm before the weather gets worse."

I watched her walk toward the parking lot with a nagging feeling in my gut.

"Tatum, wait a minute. I was wondering...would you like to grab a coffee with me tomorrow?"

She stopped and turned to look at me, a soft smile creeping over her lips. "I could be persuaded. After all, you saved me from failing my paper. Does seven tomorrow night work? I can meet you at The Coffee Bean on campus?"

"I will see you then."

We both stood looking at each other when I heard my name

called. Tearing my eyes off her long enough to look over my shoulder, I saw Elliott come jogging across the parking lot.

"Where the hell have you been? We're all waiting for you." He looked over at Tatum. "I see you met my little sister."

Light poured into the dark parking lot and brought me out of my memory. Elliott waved from the back door of the station before heading over to his car. Normally, I'd go home after a shift, but instead, I decided to hit the gym. It had been a long day, and I needed to take my frustration out on something. God, I missed her. Putting my truck into reverse, I sped out of the parking lot, looking forward to my escape.

Chapter Four

Tatum

Friday morning had finally arrived. I was looking forward to getting this day over with and having yet another weekend to mope around in bed. I walked into the lobby and headed to the washroom. My head was pounding after another night of tossing and turning.

I checked my face in the mirror. I could see the attempt to hide the dark circles under my eyes had been unsuccessful. I searched my purse for my compact and dabbed at my eyes again. It made no difference, so I threw it back in my purse. After running a brush through my hair and popping two Tylenol, I made my way upstairs."

For being the end of the month, the office was really quiet this morning. After all, we were on a deadline to get the magazine to print. After hanging my coat, I walked to my desk and turned on the computer. As soon as I sat down, I heard a knock on my door. Looking up, I saw Shelley, Mr. Keller's assistant.

"Sorry to bother you, Tatum, but Mr. Keller wants to see you in his office immediately."

I frowned. "Did he say what it was about?"

"He didn't. He just asked that I send you over as soon as you got here."

I smiled at Shelley. "Okay, let him know I will be right there." I put my purse on the floor under my desk and quickly scanned my emails to make sure there was nothing pressing. I walked down the hall and stopped outside of Mr. Keller's office. Straightening my pencil skirt, I knocked.

"It's open," I heard through the door.

Turning the handle, I peeked my head in. "Mr. Keller, Sir, you asked to see me?"

"Tatum, yes, please come in and have a seat," he said, pointing to the chair across from him. Mr. Keller put his pen down and clasped his hands on the desk.

"It's quiet around here for a Friday." I smiled, sitting in the chair across from him.

He took a deep, slow breath and exhaled. "Tatum, I am afraid I have some bad news."

I could feel the pressure building in my chest. I couldn't take much more this week. Trying to keep my breathing steady, I continued to focus on Mr. Keller and remained calm.

"There is no easy way to put it. The company is undergoing a restructure. Unfortunately, we have to lay some people off. I'm sorry, but your position is being eliminated."

I didn't know what to say. I sat there, staring at him. This week had just gone from bad to worse at a speed of ninety miles per hour.

"How long?" I kept my voice steady, even though I felt like I was going to bust. I silently prayed it wouldn't be too long.

"Right now it looks like this will be permanent. Of course, we will provide you with a recommendation letter and hope that you will come back to us if there is an opportunity in the future."

Swallowing hard, I stood from the chair. I had to get out of there. "Of course. Please, give me time to gather my belongings. I will be out of the office in the next sixty minutes."

"Of course, Tatum. Please take your time, and here is your letter." He held the envelope out for me to take, his face somber.

Reaching across the desk, I grabbed it from him, gave a slight smile and nod, and walked out of the office. I stood outside of his office against the wall, holding onto the envelope he had given me as if it was the only thing I had left on earth. What was I going to do?

The walls were starting to close in on me when Shelley came around the corner. I stood back up, nodded at her, and made my way to my office to clear out my things.

By noon, I had pretty much everything packed up when my cell phone rang. Dean's name flashed across the screen.

After all that had happened, I was in no mood to speak with him, so I let it go to voicemail.

Anxiety was creeping up on me faster than I wanted. My chest was heavy, my head fuzzy, and I was extremely dizzy. My world had come crashing down on me all at once; losing my job and my boyfriend all within one week was too much for me. The last time I felt like this was when Parker left.

The room grew dark and my breathing heavy, but I fought to gain control. Sitting down, I took a few deep breaths and sipped water from the mug on my desk.

Shelley poked her head into my office. "Is everything okay, Tatum?"

"Not really. I've been laid off. I was just gathering my thoughts before I take my things and get into the car." Taking another sip of water, I stood, steadying myself against the desk. "Would you mind helping me carry these boxes down to my car?"

"Not at all."

I smiled at her and grabbed my purse and a box while she grabbed the other one, and we walked out of the office.

I GRABBED MY MAIL AS I WALKED INTO MY APARTMENT building and headed to the elevator. I planned on ordering Chinese and drinking a couple of bottles of wine tonight. As I approached my apartment, I saw a box lying on the floor outside my door. Getting closer, I saw it was from a local florist. The little window in the box displayed about three dozen long-stem red roses. Picking it up, I opened the card on the front.

"Be mine again, Love Dean"

Rolling my eyes, I opened the apartment door. Once inside, I set the box of flowers on the counter and the rest of my stuff on the table. I removed my shoes and went to sit on the couch when someone knocked on the door.

Frowning, I checked the peephole first as I wasn't expecting anyone. Dean stood on the other side. He knocked again. I rested my head against the door, trying to decide if I should let him in. The fear of what happened the other night was still vivid in my mind. If I let him in, I didn't want to fight, and I didn't want to get hit again.

"Tatum, you there?"

Taking a deep breath, I stood back and opened the door.

"Hey sweetie." He smiled at me and stepped inside. "Did you get my flowers?"

I didn't feel like dealing with him after the day I'd had. "Yes. I don't know why you went to all the trouble."

"I was hoping we could have dinner and talk?" he suggested, holding up a bottle of wine and some takeout.

"No, Dean, I don't think so." I didn't have the patience for him.

"Please, Tatum. It has been a week. We owe it to one another to talk this through. Give us another try."

He must have lost his mind, or I had for what I was about to do. I stepped out of the way and waved him into the kitchen. Shutting the door, I followed him.

"While I get the food out, why don't you put your

flowers in a vase, sweetheart. I have to heat some of this anyway." He busied himself, grabbing plates and a couple wine glasses from the cupboard.

"Please, Dean, don't call me sweetheart. You don't mean it anyways," I mumbled under my breath as I grabbed a vase from under the counter. I would rather shred the flowers, but I filled the vase with water then cut and arranged the flowers.

One thing about Dean: he always bought gorgeous flowers, always red roses. He never spared the expense. It was probably a good thing, considering how often during the past year he had bought them for me. Who was I kidding? He was probably on some frequent-buyer program. I buried my nose in one of the roses when I felt Dean come up behind me.

Wrapping his arms around my waist, he whispered, "People make mistakes, Tatum. I want you, always have. I made a stupid mistake. I ended things with her before I left, and I came back early so I could be with you. I wanted to call you all week, but after what went on, I thought we needed some time apart."

I shrugged out of his embrace and kept reorganizing the flowers and baby's breath. He went back to plating some of the food and poured the wine. I wanted his words to be true, that he had ended it and everything including the hit was a mistake. I didn't want this night to end up being a mistake.

I jumped at the sound of Dean's cell phone ringing. "Aren't you going to answer it?" I looked over my shoulder at him.

He shook his head as he locked eyes with me. He removed his phone from his jacket pocket and turned the power off. He walked toward me and wrapped me in his embrace from behind. His cologne intoxicating; he always smelled so good.

"No distractions tonight. It's you and me." He kissed me below the ear, and then took the skin between his teeth and bit down.

I flinched. I hated when he did that. I tried to let myself relax against him as he kissed and bit the side of my neck again, and then trailed a few small, light kisses along my neck. His hands traveled down to cup my ass, and he wrapped his arm around my waist and pulled me back into him. I could feel his arousal pressing into me while he kissed down the back of my neck.

"Do you see what you do to me?" he whispered. "I'm so sorry I hurt you, baby," A soft moan escaped my lips when his hand cupped my breast. Dean turned me around and picked me up, and I wrapped my legs around his waist as he carried me to the bedroom.

I AWOKE TO THE SMELL OF COFFEE BREWING. Stretching, I climbed out of bed and headed to the living room. Dean sat on the couch, feet up on the coffee table, his phone in one hand and coffee in the other.

"Morning."

"Morning. Let me grab you a coffee." He threw his phone onto the table, and as he walked into the kitchen, his phone lit up with a text. I glanced down at the screen and saw a string of messages between Dean and someone named Tasha. I looked up, making sure he wasn't watching me before picking up the phone. I read through the last few messages on the screen.

DEAN: I'LL BE HOME SHORTLY, JUST LANDED

TASHA: GOOD, CANNOT WAIT, YOU KNOW WHERE YOU'LL FIND ME ;)

DEAN: BEST BE IN BED, NAKED WITH YOUR LEGS OPEN FOR ME BABY

My stomach started turning, and saliva built up in my mouth. I couldn't read any farther, but at the same time, I couldn't stop. I read those words over and over. I could hear my pulse loud in my ears. The smell of coffee in the room had become nauseating. Dean came around the corner and stopped dead in his tracks when he saw the expression on my face.

"What is it?"

"I can't believe I was this stupid."

"What? What are you talking about?"

Standing up, I walked over to him and held up his phone. Looking him directly in the face I spat, "Tasha is waiting for you with her legs open! You bastard! Get the fuck out."

I opened the door to my apartment and threw his phone out into the hallway. Grabbing his jacket from the back of the chair, I pushed him out the door. "Don't bother coming back here either!" I screamed as I slammed and locked the door. I couldn't believe I was so stupid. I was so angry at myself that I could barely stand to be near myself.

I checked through the peephole to make sure he had left, and then went and had a long, hot shower. I wanted nothing of him left on me. When my skin couldn't take any more scrubbing, I shut the water off and dried myself.

I grabbed the mug he had used and took it into the kitchen. Spying the roses on the counter, I walked over to the vase and dumped them all into the garbage. It was always fucking roses, and I hated them. If I never saw another red rose in my entire life, it would be too soon.

The tears started falling as I looked around the apartment. It was that moment I realized I needed a change. Nothing was holding me here anymore. Elliott was always bugging me to visit, so I'd do the next best thing and move.

I grabbed my laptop, bringing it to the dining room table I started searching for a one-way flight to Emerald Bay.

"Hey, Tatum, 'bout time you got back to me. How was your day?"

"I have a surprise for you." My voice was hoarse, but I was smiling. It was the first time I had smiled in a week.

"Is everything okay? You sound like you've been crying."

How did he do that every time? "I'm coming down with a cold, Elliott," I lied. "Do you want to know what your surprise is?" I asked, the excitement creeping back into my voice.

He laughed into the phone. "Sure, hit me."

"I booked a flight today. I'll be seeing you in three weeks!"

"Awesome! It's about time. I can't wait to see you."

I hadn't seen Elliott for a year that was the last time he was home. Before he moved, we were inseparable. Elliott continued talking about the things we would do when I arrived. I was concentrating so hard on how to tell him it was more than just a visit that I barely heard a word he said.

"Elliott, can you do me a favor before I come down?" I asked suddenly.

"Of course! What do you need?"

"Can you find me a place to live?" I swallowed hard. There was nothing but silence on the other end of the phone. "Elliott?"

"What's going on, Tatum?"

"What? I just think I could use a change of scenery. I've already booked movers." I wasn't sure if he would see through that flimsy excuse or not, and if he did, he didn't let on. I never uprooted easily, and no one knew me better than Elliott.

"Yes, of course, I will help you. If I can't find you a place before you get here, you can always stay with me for a bit."

"Sounds good. I'm going to stay with Jen for a few days."

"Okay. Listen, I have to be at work soon. I've got to go. Say hi to Jen, and call me if you need anything, okay?"

"Okay." After we hung up, I packed my bag. I had called Jen and told her I would be there shortly. I couldn't wait to get out of this apartment.

Chapter Five

Tatum - Three Weeks Later

"IS THAT EVERYTHING, MISS?" THE YOUNG MAN ASKED AS he loaded the last of the boxes onto his dolly to take out to the moving truck. I looked around my empty apartment. The only thing left to do was sweep the floors.

"I believe so, but I will double check and meet you downstairs." I was flying out on Saturday. I hoped the movers would have my stuff in Emerald Bay in time for me on Saturday night. Once I was sure all the rooms were empty, I headed down to see them off.

"Looks like that's everything," I told the young mover. My phone vibrated in my hand, and I checked the screen, Dean again. I placed the phone back in my pocket, ignoring the call.

"Did you need to take that, miss? It's been ringing all afternoon. Someone must want to get a hold of you."

I looked at him and shook my head.

"Okay, well, we will arrive in Emerald Bay by the latest Saturday evening. No worries, miss." He latched the back door shut and locked it. "Everything will arrive."

"Oh here, I almost forgot I owe the down payment." Digging into my back pocket, I pulled out a check. "We agreed the rest would be due on delivery. I just need to know what the added cost was for you to move my car so I can make out the check."

"No, miss. It's not necessary. Your bill has already been paid in full."

I stopped writing the check and looked up at him. "What? By whom?"

He searched the bottom of the invoice. "Elliott." He smiled and hopped up into the truck then passed me a copy of my invoice.

I watched as the truck drove down the road and felt my phone vibrate in my pocket again. Taking it out, I opened my text app.

DEAN: WOULD REALLY LIKE TO GET TOGETHER AND TALK.

"That's too bad," I mumbled and shoved the phone back in my pocket. An hour later, I turned my key in to the building superintendent then wheeled my suitcase out to the sidewalk to wait for the cab I'd called. I had spent most of the last three weeks with Jen and felt as if I was intruding. Tonight, I had decided to spend the night at the Radisson.

It didn't take long for the cab to pick me up and take me to the hotel. I ordered room service once I had checked in. I hadn't eaten all day, and with everything that had gone on, I was starving. I then made a call to Elliott. His phone rang twice before he answered.

"Hey, sis! How did everything go with the movers?"

"It went well, Elliott, but you didn't have to pay for it."

"I wanted that to be a surprise for you. I'm happy to do it. What time do I need to pick you up on Saturday?"

I could hear the police radio chattering in the background. I hated bothering him while he was at work.

"My flight lands around two in the afternoon on Saturday. I can take a cab. You don't have to be there to pick me up; I have the address to my new place."

"Don't even start that nonsense, Tatum."

"Elliott, I don't want to be an imposition. You found me the place, and now you've paid for my movers." I felt terrible.

"I'm going to stop you right there. I wanted to pay for them. I'm excited you're moving down, and the last thing you are to me is an imposition. I want to be there when you arrive." The line grew quiet. I wasn't going to fight him anymore. "Have you heard from him?"

"Yes, he called, but I didn't answer." I had a feeling Elliott knew I was hiding things, but I didn't want him to worry about me any more than he was.

"Good, the sooner you're away from there, the happier I will be. I don't want anything to happen to you."

I heard the radio go again in the background and heard Elliott respond.

"Listen, I gotta go. Got a call. I'll see you Saturday!"

I FELL ASLEEP AFTER DINNER. IT HAD BEEN A LONG FEW days of packing and getting everything ready, and I was exhausted.

Something startled me out of my sleep. The television was on, the room was dark, and it took me a minute to get my bearings and remember where I was. Someone was pounding on the door. I glanced at the clock on the table. Ten forty-five. What on earth? The only one who knew I was here was Jen.

Figuring it was her, I got up from the bed and went to the door. "What is up with—" It was as if all the air had been pulled out of my lungs. "Dean."

"Why haven't you returned my calls or my texts?" Pushing past me, he made his way into the room, closing the door behind him.

"Dean, what are you... How did you know I was here?"

"I have my ways." He shrugged.

"You followed me?" I questioned.

"Well, I've been calling and messaging for the past three weeks with no response. I had to do something. I don't like being ignored, Tatum."

"That's because I have nothing more to say to you, Dean." I crossed my arms over my chest and leaned against the wall.

"I finally went to your place of work today and found out you were laid off three weeks ago. Then I went to your apartment and saw you dealing with movers. I waited, parked across the street, and followed you here when you left. I'm tired of being ignored, Tatum." He pressed himself up against me, his cold eyes meeting mine. "We need to talk."

"Dean, I have nothing to say to you. I want you to leave."

"You do understand that you belong to me. I told you I made a mistake. We forgive people who make mistakes, Tatum. Now, tell me where you think you're going." He towered over me, placed both hands on the wall, one on either side of my head, and gave a threatening stare.

"It was a mistake the first time, and I forgave you. You've had your second chance, and again you lied. We're over, and you don't need to know where I'm going. You don't own me." I tried to walk away, but he grabbed hold of my arms and pinned me in place. "Dean, let go of me. You're hurting me." His grip was so strong on my arms, I could feel bruises forming.

"I have my ideas about where you are planning to go, and I don't like it. I've told you, I don't want you seeing your brother. I'm warning you to think twice about leaving."

"You're hurting me." I struggled to get out of his grip, but there was no use.

He released my left arm and ran his hand over my breast. "You still get turned on by me," he said, rolling my hardened nipple between his fingers.

I could feel my stomach start to turn.

"Don't deny your body what it wants, Tatum." He leaned in and kissed under my ear, biting my neck hard as he continued manipulating my nipple. "I bet you're wet for me." His hand moved to the button on my jeans.

"Dean, please don't." I started to cry while trying to shove him away with my free arm, but it did little good; he wouldn't budge. "We're not going to happen. We are over. Now leave!" I shouted, panicking. I hoped that I had shouted loud enough for someone in the next room to hear me and knock on the door.

"We're far from over, Tatum. Don't make me hurt you." He wrapped his hand in my hair and roughly pulled my head back. His angry eyes looked into mine as he pulled me away from the wall and led me over to the bed.

My cell phone rang. "You've already hurt me," I cried. I glared up at him and felt him finally release my hair. "I need to get that call." Keeping my eyes on him, I walked over and picked up my cell. "Elliott, I'm glad you called me back." I could hear the shake in my voice and hoped that he couldn't detect it.

Dean glared at me for what seemed like forever, and then walked out of the room, shutting the door behind him. Running over, I latched the deadbolt and let out the breath I didn't know I was holding. I leaned against the door, focusing on Elliott's voice to try and calm down.

Chapter Six

Parker

I WALKED INTO THE PUB AND SPOTTED ELLIOTT SITTING at a table near the bar. I signaled to the bartender to bring me a beer and headed over to our table. "Hey, bro, what the hell is going on?" I slapped Elliott on the back. Beer would go down easy tonight. We had finished our shift; it had been a day from hell.

"Ah, not much. Been busy. I had a pile of shit to do while we were off. I'm also very worried about Tatum." Elliott looked stressed, which was unusual for him.

"Why? What's going on?" This was not how I wanted to spend my night. I could barely keep my mind off her, since Elliott told me she would be coming down for a visit. I didn't need to know something was wrong.

"I received a call from Tatum. She started off by telling

me she was coming for a visit, but she sounded strange. Then she asked me to find her a place. That she had decided to move here."

"Just like that?" Tatum was never one to change like that.

"Yep, just like that. She hadn't even spoken to me about it and had already booked movers. I can't help but get the feeling that something is wrong, but she won't talk to me." Elliott took a long pull on his beer. "I hate being this far from her, and I hate the fact that she won't talk to me."

I grew quiet. They had always been close. For Tatum not to talk to him, it had to be bad. "What was going on with her before all this?"

"Well, she's been dating this guy who hasn't been treating her very well. I am not a fan of his to begin with. She found him with another woman, and they broke up. Then she got let go from her job, and now, she's suddenly adamant on moving down here. It's odd behavior for her."

"Maybe she really does need a change."

"No. Something isn't right."

I knew all too well what he was talking about. A waitress walked over and set our beers in front of us, the soft smell of coconut floating by as she walked away. That scent reminded me of one of my favorite, but also one of the worst, memories of Tatum.

It was the night of the beach bonfire. It was our yearly tradition with people from college. Even though we had graduated last year, we still held onto the tradition. Tatum and I stayed behind after everyone had left, the night air cold coming off the water. I wrapped my arms around her as she sat between my legs.

"Smile for me," I whispered into her ear and held my phone out in front of us and snapped our picture. I put my phone down and held her tighter in my arms. Nothing made me happier than holding her. I inhaled the smell of her, coconut invaded my senses, instantly making me hard. I bent down and kissed her on the neck, and she turned and met my mouth with hers.

I lay back, pulling her down beside me, and covered her bare legs with the spare blanket. I kissed her, my tongue exploring her mouth as she let out a soft moan. My hand ran from her knee up under her skirt and gently rubbed her thigh. She spread her legs for me. Moving my hand, I rubbed her wet panties, pressing just hard enough for her to feel me.

"Feel good?" I whispered.

She bit her bottom lip and shyly nodded, the blush rising to her cheeks. God, I loved that look on her. Pushing her panties to the side, I ran my finger through her wetness from her opening to her clit, then rubbed her in tiny, slow circles. Kissing her, I slipped one finger deep inside her, and then another while I rubbed her clit with the pad of my thumb. She let out a low moan into my mouth. I loved the feel of her warm, wet walls around my fingers.

It wasn't long before she came, her body relaxing. She lay in my arms afterward and we watched the stars. I was in love with her. It was always so easy with her.

It was almost one when I dropped her off at the apartment she shared with her brother. When I got home, there was a message from the police recruiting agency. I had gotten the job with the Emerald Bay Police Department and I had forty-eight hours to respond. The next afternoon, armed with an engagement ring in my pocket, I went over to see my girl.

"Man, did you hear anything I said?" Elliott waved, snapping me out of my memory.

"What?" I must have looked like an idiot. Here I was, sitting across from her brother, remembering the last night I was with his sister. Thank God he couldn't see below the table; my painful erection was straining against my jeans.

"She arrives tomorrow," he repeated.

I shifted in my seat, doing my best to readjust myself. I nodded to the bartender for another round as I took a long swig, emptying my beer. It was going to be a long night.

"Aren't you working for me tomorrow?" I asked.

"Yes." He hesitated. "Parker, I have a huge favor to ask."

He was crazy if he thought I would pick her up. There was no way I could do that. I wasn't ready to see her.

"I hate to ask, but would you be able to pick her up for me and bring her to this address? I'll be done with work at four but won't be able to get there for two."

He scratched out an address on a napkin and passed it over to me.

"I don't want her to have to take a cab from the airport."

I frowned as I looked down at the address he had written. It was about a block from my place. What the hell! It had taken me the last eight years to even think about dating seriously again. The past few years had been nothing but one-night stands, and I was growing tired of it now. I wanted more—I needed more—and now the girl I had never gotten over would be living less than a five-minute drive from my place. I took in a deep breath. I must have lost my mind.

"What time?"

"Her flight lands at two. Gate B4," Elliott informed.

I placed the napkin in my pocket and ordered us some food. "I'll be back. Gonna hit the bathroom."

Standing outside the washroom, I pulled my cell phone out of my pocket. Opening my contacts, I pulled Tatum's information up on my screen. I wanted to text her. Hell, I had wanted to text her every time I got drunk. Every time I was lonely and horny, and pretty much every day for the last eight fucking years. My finger hovered over the text icon for what seemed like hours, but I decided against it. I slid my phone back into my pocket and went back out to drown my sorrows in more beer.

Chapter Seven

Tatum

JEN PULLED UP OUTSIDE THE AIRPORT AND HANDED THE valet her keys. After Dean left me in my hotel room, I checked out and went to stay with her. As I went to get out of the car, my phone chimed as Dean's name flashed across the screen.

"God, he is messaging me again! When is he going to get it through his head we are over?" I said as Jen pulled my suitcase out of the trunk.

"I think you need to change your number. Have you mentioned anything to Elliott about what happened?"

"Are you crazy? Elliott would lose his mind if he knew what Dean has done. I'll change my number once the move is complete."

"Elliott needs to know about this. The bastard hit you

and then attacked you. You should be pressing charges on his ass."

"I know, but I swear, aside from the day I caught him with that woman, he has never laid a hand on me." That wasn't exactly the truth, but I didn't want her to know any different.

"Take a look at yourself. You're covered in bruises." She glanced at my arms. "Elliott needs to know, Tatum, and you know if he finds out by seeing these marks on you, he will be pissed. Who is to say Dean won't find you and come after you, have you thought about that? I'm worried about you, Tatum. You're my best friend." She placed her hand on my arm, the look in her eyes saying it all.

"Everything will be fine." I didn't want to let on that I was also afraid of him finding me, so I did my best to ignore her comment. "Besides, Dean doesn't even know where I'm going."

"You told me he said he has an idea. That scares me! He could be following us right now." Jen looked around the parking lot.

I looked at her and sighed. "I promise when I get settled, the first thing I will do is get myself a new number and maybe an alarm system."

Jen sighed, her eyes running to the bruises on my arms. "You're also going to talk to your brother!"

"I'll be fine! Stop worrying!"

"I'm not convinced, Tatum. You were so scared when you arrived last night, and your phone hasn't stopped going off since. I hope you're telling me the truth, that a new number will be the first thing on your agenda when you get there."

"I promise. Now let's go so I can check in.

"All right, I will take you as far as they will allow, and then you will only be waiting for an hour before boarding. At least I know that you will be safe here."

After I checked in for my flight, we stopped at a little cafe for a coffee. Jen ran over to the nearest washroom while I grabbed us a table. I took a quick minute while she was gone to check my messages. Fifteen messages from Dean, this morning alone, and they were still coming in. I felt the color drain from my face when I reached the most recent text. It sent chills through me.

DEAN: YOU THINK YOU CAN GET AWAY FROM ME. I WANT YOU TO KNOW YOU CAN'T HIDE FROM ME. WE WILL BE TOGETHER AGAIN SOON. HOPE YOU ENJOY THAT COFFEE SITTING IN FRONT OF YOU.

I sat staring at my phone. I was so scared that I didn't even hear Jen come back to the table.

"Tatum, you don't look very good. What is it?"

I handed my phone to Jen who read over the screen.

"He is scaring me, Tatum. Please talk to Elliott."

Ignoring her plea, I took a drink of my coffee. "Did I tell you who Elliott is partnered with?" I was trying to change the subject.

Jen shook her head no as she took a sip of her tea.

"Parker."

She stopped mid-sip to look at me.

"You heard me," I said.

"Parker? As in, your ex-boyfriend from college, the love of your life, that Parker?"

I answered her with a nod, a warm feeling coming over me.

"Have you spoken to him at all since you found out?"

"No. But apparently they hang out a lot, so I'm guessing I'll see him when I get there."

"Maybe that's a good thing, if you get my drift." She waggled her eyebrows.

I giggled. "Don't get your hopes up. That was a long, long time ago. Besides, he is probably married now with a couple of kids." I looked at my watch as I took my last mouthful of coffee.

"Yeah, but aren't you the least bit curious?" She smiled at me.

I *was* curious. Parker had rarely left my mind in the years following our breakup. Having regrets was the worst feeling in the world.

"Maybe a little curious, but I'm not going down there to get involved with anyone. I better get going." I looked at my watch again. "I still have to go through security. I will text you as soon as I land." I gave Jen a hug. "Thanks for everything these last few weeks. I appreciate you letting me crash with you."

"I'm going to miss you." She hugged me again. "Please remember to talk to Elliott."

We walked over to the gate and said a final good-bye. I headed toward the security check point and handed them my passport and boarding pass. I couldn't wait to get started with my new life.

I WOKE UP AND STRETCHED AS THE PLANE TOUCHED down. It had been a quiet flight, and the best gift was my phone on airplane mode so Dean couldn't bother me. I managed to get a couple hours of sleep which I was in desperate need of. I had a feeling there would be a slew of texts and messages from him waiting for me once I turned my phone back on. I was trying not to worry about it, but my anxiety was getting the better of me.

I reached down and picked my purse up off the floor and unbuckled my belt. I was stiff from being crammed up against the side of the plane. As soon as we were able, I stood and grabbed my only bag from the overhead carrier and made my way to the exit. Thanking the flight attendant, I made my way down the ramp toward customs, and then to the designated meeting area.

Searching the crowd of people for Elliott, I felt a little discouraged when I didn't see him right away. Figuring he may have gotten delayed, I grabbed a coffee from the closest shop.

"I'll take a large coffee with coconut milk and honey please." I reached into my purse, grabbed my phone, and turned my data back on. After I paid, I went to sit down at one of the little tables outside the coffee cubicle. I immediately noticed Elliott's name highlighted on my phone and clicked on the message.

ELLIOTT: SORRY, TATUM. I WORK UNTIL FOUR, BUT I'VE ARRANGED FOR PARKER TO PICK YOU UP WHEN YOUR FLIGHT LANDS. I'M SORRY. I WANTED TO BE THERE. PLEASE TEXT ME ONCE YOU HAVE LANDED.

I looked around at the crowds. Parker must be late, too. I swallowed down the nerves I felt building in my stomach —the same feeling I had the night Elliott told me he was working with him—at the thought of seeing Parker after all these years. I took a sip of my coffee and concentrated on breathing deeply while waiting for him to arrive.

Chapter Eight

Parker

I STOOD ACROSS FROM THE EXIT AT GATE B4 AND watched Tatum. She looked exactly like I remembered. Her soft blonde hair brushed the side of her neck—hair I had longed to run my fingers through again. And her ass still looked amazing in her yoga pants.

My breath hitched and desire ran through me. I felt myself grow hard. I needed to get air before I went to talk to her. I looked down at my watch. I was already late. A half hour late to be exact, Elliott was going to kill me. I should have made something up to get out of this. Who had I been kidding? I wasn't prepared to see her, even after all this time.

I went to walk outside to get some air when I felt my

phone vibrate in my pocket. Pulling out my phone, I saw a message from Elliott.

ELLIOTT: WHERE YOU AT? TATUM IS WAITING FOR YOU. SHE HAS BEEN WAITING FOR FORTY-FIVE MINUTES.

I closed my eyes, took a deep breath, and swallowed hard. Typing out a quick response to Elliott, I turned and headed back into the airport.

I walked up behind her, cleared my throat, and softly said her name.

She turned, and I met those gorgeous hazel eyes that I had missed so much.

"Parker?" A smile came across her face. "Oh my God!"

She stood up and wrapped her arms around me, pressing her body into mine. She still smelled like coconut. Wrapping my arms around her, I pulled her in tighter and inhaled. It felt good to have her in my arms again, and I prayed she couldn't feel the hard ridge in my pants.

"I'm just going to grab a quick coffee. Have a seat," I said, guiding Tatum to sit back down.

I had spent five minutes in line listening to some woman ream out the barista because she had gotten her order wrong when I finally got my coffee. I walked back to the table and sat down across from her. "How have you been, Tatum?"

She looked exhausted and pale, and her eyes were bloodshot and lined with dark circles.

"I've been okay, Parker. What about you?"

I loved the way my name rolled off her tongue, and I would especially love to hear her scream my name. I had to stop thinking of her like this now. I shifted in my seat, the throbbing between my legs getting worse.

"Doing well. Elliott must have told you I am his partner now. I trained him when he started on this unit. Sure is a small world isn't it?" I looked up at her. She was looking down at the screen on her cell phone, completely ignoring what I had just said. The little color she had was now completely drained from her face. "Tatum? Is something wrong?"

"Hmmm...?"

"Is something wrong?" I raised my voice a little.

"It's nothing." She gave me a funny look, as if she was hiding something. Putting her cell into her purse, she said, "What do you say we get going?"

"What's the hurry? Relax, drink your coffee."

I watched as she looked through the crowd anxiously, fidgeting with her coffee cup. At one point, I thought I caught a glimpse of fear in her eyes.

"Tatum, are you sure everything is okay?" I didn't want to pry, but Elliott had been right, she was acting very strange, as if she was afraid of something. I hadn't seen her in years, and even I could tell.

She leaped up out of her seat and disposed of her coffee. Grabbing her bag and purse, she started heading toward the closest exit.

I frowned. She had no idea where I had even parked.

I grabbed my coffee and called after her, but she didn't stop. When she finally slowed her pace, I ran up beside her and grabbed hold of her upper arm. I saw her flinch at my touch, and I pulled my hand away. "Is everything all right? Did I hurt you?"

"No, you didn't hurt me. I'm fine."

"What on earth has you moving so quickly? You don't even know where I'm parked." She was avoiding my eyes which made me feel uneasy. She was definitely running from something.

When she finally met my eyes, she looked as if she could cry. "It's nothing, Parker. Just tired and emotional I guess. It's been a long few weeks. Guess everything is finally catching up with me. I'm just glad to finally be here."

I watched her expressions. She wasn't telling me the truth either. Elliott was right. Whatever had happened was pretty bad, but I had to shrug it off. After all, I hadn't seen her in years. I didn't expect her to tell me anything.

"Okay then, let's head to your new place."

Taking her bag from her, we turned in the direction of the parking garage. Once we reached my truck, I helped her up into the front seat and loaded her bag into the back seat. It wasn't long before we were on the road heading to the address that Elliott had given me.

TATUM

ONCE WE LEFT THE AIRPORT PARKING LOT AND PULLED

out onto the highway, I finally started to relax. I kept stealing quick glances of Parker. His dark hair used to be long and always pulled up into a man bun, but was now cut pretty tight. His strong jaw line was more prominent with the beard he now wore, and his blue shirt enhanced his blue eyes. I watched as his strong hands gripped the steering wheel and his forearms flexed. I couldn't help but wonder what it would be like to have those hands on me. I clenched my thighs, trying to calm my throbbing center. Needing air, I reached over and rolled the window down. He had always been attractive, but time had turned him into a man.

"Did you want me to put the air on, Tatum?"

"No, I'm okay, thanks. I wanted some fresh air."

Giving a small, sexy smile, he turned his gaze back to the road. I wasn't sure how much longer I could be in this truck with him. I felt as if I was going to explode.

After what felt like hours, we finally pulled up in front of my new home. I saw my car parked in the driveway in front of Elliott's truck. The house was a small, blue bungalow right on the bay. I was already in love.

"He picked a good area for you, Tatum. There is a very low crime rate here. Also, you're not too far from Elliott... or me for that matter," Parker said, putting the truck in park.

I stepped out of the truck just as the front door to my new home opened. Elliott came strolling down the front walkway still dressed in his uniform. I ran to give him a hug.

"Elliott this is perfect!" I said, wrapping my arms around him. "I love it!"

"Well, if you love it from seeing it out here, I'm sure you will love the inside." He grinned, letting me go and waving to Parker. "Hey, man, thanks for picking her up." Elliott walked over and got my bag and purse from the back seat of Parker's truck.

I stood and watched from a distance as Parker declined coming in. He said his good-byes to Elliott, gave a wave, one hell of a sexy smile to me, and pulled away from the curb. A part of me was kind of glad that Parker didn't stay. The man was walking sex. From the moment I had laid eyes on him in the airport, I was instantly wet. I couldn't stop wondering what it would be like to lay beneath him and feel the weight of his body on mine. He even smelled the same. I watched as Parker drove away.

Elliott stood in front of me, looking in the same direction. "I hope that wasn't too uncomfortable for you?"

I shrugged. "It was a little, but I got through it. It was nice to see him."

Elliott put his hand on my back and turned to guide me toward the house. "Are you ready to go in and see your new place? The movers arrived yesterday, so everything is here." Elliott led the way into the house, carrying my bag.

It was a two-bedroom house with a decent-sized living room and a galley kitchen—more than enough space for me. I had planned on doing some writing and decided to use the smaller of the two bedrooms for an office. The bedroom and living room had a sliding door leading out to the back deck overlooking the bay. It would be a perfect place to drink my morning coffee and get some sun. My bedroom held my king-size bed perfectly. This house couldn't be more perfect.

"Elliott, I love it."

"Great, I'm glad. Did you want to get out and grab a bite? I could take you to get some groceries as well before I head home."

"Sounds great! I'm starving." I washed up and grabbed my purse, and then locked the door behind me as we headed to get some food.

Chapter Nine

Tatum

Elliott had dropped me off around nine, after helping me in with my groceries. Once he was gone, I noticed how quiet the house was. I stopped putting everything away. I needed some type of noise.

Elliott had spent some time hooking up the TV in the living room and bedroom, so I went and put the TV on. I heard my cell go off in my purse and realized I hadn't checked my messages all day, which meant I hadn't sent Jen a text to let her know I had arrived safely. She was going to be freaking out.

Grabbing my phone, I typed my password in, and another message from Dean flashed across my screen. My shoulders tensed as I read it.

DEAN: IF YOU THINK YOU'VE ESCAPED ME, YOU'RE DEAD WRONG. I'LL BE COMING TO FIND YOU. I CAN'T WAIT TO FEEL MYSELF BURIED DEEP INSIDE OF YOU AGAIN.

I felt sick. I wanted no reminders of him at all, so I erased all his messages from my phone and typed out a message to Jen. My phone started ringing seconds later, and Jen's face popped up on my screen.

"Thanks for messaging. I've been worried sick about you. How's everything?" she blurted as soon as I picked up.

"Hey, Jen! Yeah, I'm sorry about that. It's been a long, busy day."

"How was the flight? Did Elliott pick you up on time?"

"No."

"What do you mean?"

I let out a tiny laugh. "Elliott didn't pick me up. Parker did."

"Well, well, well. Is he like you remembered or did he get all fat and ugly?" I could hear the laughter in her voice.

"Does it really matter?" I grew quiet. He had bulked up considerably since the last time I had seen him. I remembered the way his T-shirt stretched across his muscles. My center began throbbing at the thought.

"Really, you know, I was thinking...you guys were always so good together. We all thought you should have gone with him when he moved, even Elliott."

I frowned. "What are you saying, Jen?"

"I just think that it's never too late to give something another try? Is he available?"

Inwardly, I winced. I'd always known our breakup was a mistake. But to find out your best friend and your brother agreed didn't make it easier.

"Jen, I told you I didn't come down here to get involved with anyone. So it doesn't matter if he is available or not."

Jen knew me well—too well—and I was sure she already knew I didn't mean the words I had just said.

"So are you telling me that if he made a move on you, you would turn him down?"

I could feel the heat rise in my cheeks at the mere thought. "I'm not even going to dignify that question with an answer."

"That's what I thought you'd say. It's okay, though, because I know the true answer."

I stood there in the kitchen, biting my lip.

"It's sad that you can't admit the truth to yourself, Tatum."

"Jen, please let this go."

"How's the new place?"

"Wait until you see it. You're going to fall in love with it. It couldn't be more perfect. You're still planning to come down in a month, right?" I questioned while pulling the kettle and a mug from one of the boxes in the kitchen and plugging it in to make a cup of tea.

"Of course, you know I'll be there." Jen got quiet for second and cleared her throat. "Tatum, I don't mean to sound like a broken record," she said, her voice growing serious.

"Then don't." I knew what was coming, and I didn't feel like listening to it.

"Have you talked to Elliott about what happened between Dean and you?"

I closed my eyes. I wanted nothing more than to forget about him. About all of it—about him hitting me and attacking me in that room and lying to me that night in my apartment. I hadn't even shared that part with Jen because I felt like a fool for thinking he wasn't still cheating on me.

"No, I haven't, and to be honest, I don't plan to. I've moved here to leave that part of my life behind, and that is what I plan to do. Elliott worries about me enough. I think it's unnecessary to add to that worry." I knew her heart was in the right place, but she needed to let it go already.

"Well, I wasn't going to tell you, but I think you should know. I am almost positive that I saw Dean at the airport when I was leaving. That message he sent you while we were there having coffee? He was watching us. Has he messaged you since you arrived?"

I was losing my patience. I knew she cared about me, and I was trying to keep that in mind. "I promise you, if he contacts me in any way before I get a new phone, I will tell Elliott. Do you feel better?" I poured the boiling water into my mug and headed into the living room to watch TV.

"I guess. I just hope you really will talk to him. I'm sure you're tired, so I'm going to let you go. You better call me soon."

We said our good-byes, and when I hung up, I shut my cell phone off. As I sat watching TV, I couldn't help but feel exposed. The first thing I was doing tomorrow was putting up curtains, I thought to myself, looking out the window.

Making sure the front and back doors were locked, I made my way into my bedroom and crawled into bed. The noises were strange in the house. The fact that I had no curtain over the sliding door in my bedroom was driving me crazy.

Getting up out of bed, I took my old comforter and hung it up over the old curtain rod that was still attached to the wall. Feeling a little more secure with the small change, I crawled back into bed and nodded off to sleep.

Chapter Ten

Parker

I GRABBED MY WET TOWEL, SHOVED IT INTO MY BAG AND headed out of the changing room. I had hit the weights hard today. I needed to release some work stress, but most importantly, I needed to rid my mind of that sexy little thing I had picked up yesterday. That sexy little thing had caused me to toss and turn all night. She was all I could think of.

As I walked up to the front desk, my gaze immediately fell on Tatum. She sat at Don's desk, her hand under her chin, looking very annoyed. Don had gone through pretty much every woman in this gym since he had started working here and loved nothing more than new meat.

I dropped my bag on the ground beside her. She jumped and her hand went to her throat as she whirled around. She seemed to relax when her eyes finally met mine, and she gave me a full smile.

"Are you getting a membership here?"

"I am. Do you work out here as well?"

"I do. Been here about three years I guess. Is Don looking after you here?" I questioned, giving Don a glare. I could tell from the look in his eyes that he had been up to his usual shit, and I knew he was afraid of me, so letting him know that I knew her pretty much guaranteed he'd stay away. "Make sure you give her my discount."

Don nodded and keyed something into the computer.

"That isn't necessary," she said to Don.

He looked up at me and excused himself from the desk.

I sat down beside her. "I stopped here because I wanted to make sure Don wasn't trying to sweep you off your feet."

"My God! You're as bad as my brother! I can take care of myself, Parker." She fidgeted in her seat.

"I never said you couldn't. Listen, I'm free until two. How about we grab a coffee as soon as you're done here?"

Tatum nodded at the idea, and once the papers were all signed, we headed over to the coffee shop.

"Two iced coffees please."

While I stood waiting for our drinks, I couldn't help looking over at Tatum. She was so cute in her sunflower sundress. It accentuated all the right places. She was still so attractive, and I couldn't help but wonder what it would feel like to kiss those lips. I watched as she ran her hand through her hair, her soft blonde locks falling back into place. How I longed to run my hands through that hair.

"Sir? Sir, your coffees."

I turned and took the coffees from the girl behind the counter. "Thanks."

I sat down beside Tatum and held her coffee in front of her. Reaching to take it from me, her fingers touched mine, sending a warm feeling straight to my groin. "Hope you like it. It's one of my favorites—a coconut iced coffee."

I watched her mouth as she took a sip, her hazel eyes closing and opening with delight. I hoped one day I would be the one to make her light up like that.

"That's really good. Thank you. It's been a long while since I had an iced coffee. So fill me in on what's gone on with you in the past eight years."

"Not much. Just work really. Police work is a pretty lonely life—lots of overtime here. I became a training officer a couple of years after I was hired. After working uniform for a few years, I was transferred to the under-cover unit. Of all people, Elliott was actually my first trainee in that unit, and now we are partners."

She looked down at her mug, and I caught a hint of sadness in her eyes. "If it's a lonely life, then I'm glad I didn't join you," she whispered, still looking down. "I take it your wife spends a lot of time alone then?" She looked up at me, and I saw the question dancing in her eyes.

My gaze traveled down her body, noticing the light bruising on both her biceps, and I frowned. Where had she gotten those from? Elliott was right, something definitely was going on, and she wasn't talking. I wanted to ask but thought it best I didn't.

"Actually, I never ended up getting married."

"Well, then your girlfriend must hate being alone all the time."

"No girlfriend either, Tatum," I said, looking away. "After you, I felt it was easier to stay single. Less hurt that way." With that admittance, I avoided her eyes.

I felt her hand on mine and looked up to see her watching me. She rubbed my hand and squeezed. "I'm sorry, Parker. I needed time. It was too much, too fast. Everything was changing. If I can be honest, sometimes I wonder if maybe I should have given us more time. Things might be different now."

I could tell she meant every word. "What about you? Are you seeing anyone?"

"I was dating this guy, but I broke it off with him. There were too many differences between us. But I'm sure Elliott told you all about it."

"He did mention something about it. What made you decide to move down here?" Again the sadness flashed in her eyes. I didn't want her to dwell on that ass.

"Well, my luck got worse. The same week we broke up, I was permanently laid off from my job. I was supposed to be coming down to visit, but with nothing really holding me there, I decided that a change of scenery might be best for me. I made a call to Elliott and told him I was going to move down, and here I am."

She took another sip of her coffee and set the cup down on the table. My gaze fell to her arm again, and I gently ran my hand over the bruises. "How did you get these?"

I watched her shift uncomfortably in her seat. Just

from the look in her eyes, I could tell she didn't want to talk about it, but I wanted to know.

"They're nothing. Don't worry about it." She brushed my hand away.

"They don't look like nothing. This is why you flinched when I grabbed your arm the other day at the airport, isn't it?"

"Don't worry about these," she said, nodding toward her arms. "They really are nothing."

"If they are nothing, then why not tell me how you got them?"

Her gaze went directly to the cup in front of her and stayed there. I could see her eyes start to fill with tears. I didn't mean to sound as if I was questioning her, but fuck, I was sure this guy had put his hands on her! For whatever reason, it never took me long to pick up on an abused woman. And for reasons I will never understand, they always covered for these deadbeats. I was trying to remain calm and not get agitated with her. I was afraid she was going to get pissed off with me, and that was the last thing I wanted. I wanted her to know she could talk to me.

"Can I ask you a question?"

She slowly nodded her head but kept her eyes on the table.

"Are you okay? Please tell me he is leaving you alone and that you aren't actually running from him."

She chewed the side of her mouth, and a dark look came over her. A single tear ran down her cheek. Reaching across the table, I wiped away the stray tear with my thumb. I wanted to make it all go away for her, but I couldn't even begin to help her if she wouldn't talk to me. I waited for a response, but she said nothing.

"How about I take you home." I stood up and grabbed the empty cups off the table and threw them out. We walked over to my truck and climbed in. "Give me your phone." I held my hand out and waited for her to place it in my hand.

She reached into her purse and pulled her phone out then slowly raised her eyes to mine. It was as if she was afraid to even look at me. This guy had done a number on her, and it pissed me right the fuck off. She looked more beat down than she did when her parents passed.

She placed her phone in my hand. I typed my name into the contacts, and my old information populated on the screen. I was a little surprised she still had me in her phone after all this time. I changed my number and handed her phone back to her.

"Give me a call or shoot me a text if you need anything or if you're lonely. I live about three blocks from you."

When she took the phone from me her fingers grazed the palm of my hand, her touch sending a jolt through me.

When I dropped her off, I waited in the driveway until I was sure she was safely inside. As I watched her walk into the house, I hoped I would hear from her sooner rather than later.

Chapter Eleven

Tatum

I rolled onto my back and stretched. Looking at the clock, I noticed it was still early, too early to get up out of bed. I relaxed back into my pillows and took in the quiet —something I rarely got to do when I was working. It had been three weeks in my new house, and everything was unpacked and arranged the way I wanted. I had even sent out resumes to some magazines and a local newspaper, but I hadn't heard anything yet. I also had the time to get my cell number changed, and thankfully I had heard nothing from Dean.

Climbing out of bed, I pulled the curtains to the side and opened the sliding door. The warm breeze blew over my body, and I could hear wind chimes in the distance. I could see a couple of sail boats already out on the bay. The leaves were already starting to change color too. The red and fire-orange leaves looked amazing against the ever-greens. I headed into the kitchen and made a cup of coffee then headed back out on the deck with my book and cell phone.

It was a beautiful morning, the birds were chirping, and a couple of people were already walking down on the beach. I sat back in my lounge chair and took a sip of my coffee. Things were finally coming together. I opened my book and began reading when my phone rang.

"Hello?"

"I see you changed your number. Did you really think that was going to stop me?" My chest tightened with fear at the sound of the deep, commanding voice on the other end of the phone.

"How did you get this number?" Elliott, Parker, and Jen were the only ones I had shared it with.

"Still questioning, I see. How many fucking times do I need to tell you not to question me? Never mind how I got your number. I want to see you," he demanded.

"Why?" My heart pounded. I was barely able to breathe.

"Again? Really? You never learn." His rough voice poured through the phone.

"Please leave me alone."

"It's not going to happen, Tatum. You're mine. Have you forgotten that already?"

I tried hard to calm the shake in my hand, my stomach starting to turn at an alarming rate. I swallowed down the massive buildup of saliva in my mouth and prayed that I didn't throw up. My memory quickly went to the night in the hotel when he assaulted me, and my blood ran cold. Why didn't I do as Jen suggested and tell Elliott?

"I have a good idea of where you are, Tatum. I'll come to get you. Don't make this harder on yourself than it needs to be. I refuse to let you go. You will be mine again."

I ended the call and tried to slow my breathing as fear clawed its way through me. Within seconds, my phone rang. It was him again, only this time I didn't answer it. Once I calmed down, I listened to the voicemail.

"You bitch. How dare you hang up on me? Keep your eyes open and watch your back. You'll never know when I'll come for you, but when I do, you can bet your ass that it's not going to be pretty."

After I listened to the voicemail, I sat on the deck, rocking back and forth in my lounge chair, my coffee having gone cold a long time ago. I decided that I needed help. I was in over my head, and it was time to tell Elliott what had been going on.

I dialed his number and waited for him to answer.

ELLIOTT AND PARKER SAT IN THEIR UNIFORMS AT MY kitchen table with a cup of coffee. When I had called Elliott, he had finished his shift and was waiting for Parker to return to the station. They had carpooled together, so they came straight over.

"What's going on? You sounded panicked on the phone," Elliott said, looking at me with concern.

"I have something to tell you, but you have to promise me that you won't get angry. I need your help." I couldn't look either of them in the eyes. I felt awful. I should have told Elliott about this a long time ago.

Elliott looked from me to Parker and chuckled. "Why do I have the sinking feeling that what I'm about to hear is going to piss me off?"

I looked from my cup to Elliott, then Parker, and back to my cup, chewing on my bottom lip. He was going to be angry, I knew it, but he had to know. "Remember how I told you about my breakup with Dean?"

"Yes, you broke it off, and you left him at the hotel."

"Well, that is sort of the truth, except for one thing."

"And what is that?" I could feel his eyes on me, and it was making me uncomfortable.

"He hit me after I confronted him."

"He laid his hands on you?"

I put my hand on Elliott's arm. "He did, but I left after he hit me."

"And after that you never saw him again, correct?" Elliott questioned.

"Not exactly." I held my head down, looking into my cup.

Elliott looked up at me with a frown. "What do you mean by not exactly, Tatum?"

"Well, he came by my apartment when he got back into town the following Saturday. He wanted to talk and see if we could work things out."

"And you better tell me that you told him to fuck right off!"

I stared down at the floor, unable to look at him. I could feel the blush from my embarrassment crawl up my face. I didn't want to answer his question, but I knew I had to.

"Tatum? Please tell me you told him to fuck off." His hands were balled into fists.

"Not exactly. He swore to me it was over between them and that he had made a huge mistake. We sort of ended up sleeping together."

Parker shifted in his seat, a look between jealousy and hate coming over his face.

Elliott slammed his fist on the table, causing me to jump. "You did *what*? I can't believe after you saw him with another woman that you would do that. What the fuck is the matter with you?" Elliott got up from his seat and walked to the other side of the room. "Wait, is that the night you called me and told me you were moving down here?"

Nodding my head, I swallowed hard, trying to keep myself from crying. "I don't know why I did it. It didn't matter anyway, because he lied to me. He was still seeing her. I found his cell phone--there were text messages still going on between them that morning."

Elliott poured himself another cup of coffee. "Did you honestly think that he was going to tell you the truth? Guys like that, Tatum, are wastes of skin. Fuck, I never liked him from the fucking start! I never should have let you talk me out of doing a background check on him when

I fucking wanted to. What else?" He put his coffee down so hard, it spilled on the table. He was pissed, and I couldn't say I blamed him.

"Well, after I talked to you that night, I went to stay with Jen. Dean started persistently calling me. Jen was sure that she saw him at the airport the day I was leaving. He has been texting me daily since I got here. Jen was adamant that I get a new number when I got here, so I did as she suggested, but he's somehow gotten it. He called me right before I called you this morning."

"You mean to tell me that Jen knows about all of this, but you wouldn't tell me? Your own brother who might actually be able to do something about this? Fuck, Tatum, I'm beyond pissed with you right now! How many times has he hit you?"

"It was only that one time." I zipped up the sweater I was wearing and averted my eyes. At this point, I didn't dare tell him that it had been happening from the beginning. I also didn't want to let him know that it had gotten worse as the year progressed.

Parker looked up from his mug and made eye contact with me, a warm look coming over his face. I could tell he felt sorry for me. He placed a hand on Elliott's shoulder. "I think the right thing to do here is not to get mad at your sister. She made a mistake. I think the fact that she's coming to you now is what's important."

Elliott ran his hands over his face and took in a deep breath. He looked between the two of us and then got up from the table and leaned against the counter. He stood with his hand on the back of his neck for a few minutes, completely quiet, just staring at the floor. "Where is this message he left you?"

I grabbed my phone and played the message for them. I hated hearing his voice; it sent chills through me. When the message was over, I sat there looking at my phone. "I'm scared, Elliott."

"Well, don't be scared. I'll look into this guy. But in the meantime, you have both of us that you can call. Parker is closer to you, so if it is an emergency, call him first, and then call me. I am going to be out of town for the next two days for a course. Keep your doors locked and make sure you always have your cell on you when you leave the house. We can get that number changed again for you."

I leaned over and wrapped my arms around my brother's neck. "Thank you for everything. I'm sorry that I didn't talk to you sooner," I whispered, kissing him on the cheek.

"You should never be afraid to talk to me, Tatum. None of what has gone on is your fault, despite how it may feel. Remember that. This guy is a problem, but you've got to tell me the truth if you need my help. I really hope you're not hiding anything else from me." He hugged me back.

As I hugged Elliott, I looked over his shoulder at Parker. He caught my glance and mouthed "tell him" as he looked to my arms. But I said nothing.

The guilt started to fall over me after they left. I should have told Elliott everything. Especially about the night before my flight when Dean showed up at the hotel, but I felt he was already angry enough. I prayed that Dean didn't follow through with his threats. I just wanted to move on with my life and be done with him. I hoped that if I wished hard enough, he would disappear, but things don't seem to work out that way.

Chapter Twelve

Tatum

I HAD FINISHED PAYING MY LAST BILL AND HEADED TO the kitchen. I still felt bad for hiding everything from Elliott, but he swore he forgave me. I prayed I wouldn't have to tell him what else I hid from him.

Placing all the dirty dishes from dinner into the dishwasher I washed down the counters then made myself some tea. A knock on the front door made me jump. I stopped what I was doing and went to the door, pulling it open. The front porch was empty. There wasn't even a car in sight.

I shrugged, grabbed the newspaper off my stoop, and shut and locked the door, turning on the outside light. I went back to cleaning, and when I was finished, I grabbed my tea and shut off the kitchen light, then headed into the living room and curled up on the couch.

Again, there was a knock at the front door. Frowning, I placed my tea on the table and went back to the door, this time looking out the peephole first. I saw no one. Fear overtook me, and I could hear my heart beating in my ears. I took a minute to try and calm myself and latched the deadbolt.

Walking into the living room, I could see a couple people down on the beach. I locked the sliding door. Elliott had installed another lock for me on both the sliding doors for added protection, so I locked those as well and pulled the curtains across the doors and windows. I loved all the windows and doors in the daytime but felt severely violated by the time darkness fell.

I shut off the lights and walked into the bedroom. Going to the sliding door, I latched both locks and pulled those curtains closed as well. I turned on the bedside light and changed into my tank top and shorts when I heard another knock on the front door.

My heart was beating rapidly in my chest. "What the hell?" I mumbled to myself.

The knocking turned into pounding, and then whoever it was started rattling the doorknob. I grabbed my cell phone and dialed Parker, the pounding getting progressively harder and more erratic.

"Harrison." His throaty voice hit me right in my center.

"Parker, it's Tatum." I could hear the shake in my voice and knew he could hear it as well.

"What's wrong?"

"Parker, can you come over? I'm scared. Someone is pounding on my front door."

"I'm on my way. Whatever you do, don't answer the door. Stay where you are until you hear from me." And like that, he was gone.

Sitting beside my bed, I pulled my knees into my chest and listened to a *Friends* rerun. I was trying to put all my concentration on the TV when suddenly, the pounding on the door stopped.

I was about to get up to go and look out the front of the house when I saw a shadow on my bedroom curtain. My heartbeat was so rapid, I was having a hard time breathing and felt as if I could pass out.

I sent Parker a text and let him know that the person was at the back of the house when lights shone through my front bedroom window. *Thank God, he's here.*

My phone chimed. "Stay put until I text you."

I waited, still sitting on the floor. It seemed like forever before my phone started to ring.

"Come to the front door and let me in. Whoever it was is gone."

I got up off the floor, still shaking, and ran to open the front door. Parker stepped inside, took one look at me, and wrapped his arms around me. I felt myself melt into his embrace.

"It's okay. You're okay." Parker held onto me as I began to cry.

PARKER WAS OUT ON THE DECK WHILE I MADE A POT OF coffee and poured us two mugs. When I stepped out the back door, I noticed Parker relaxing on one of the lounge chairs. I placed our mugs on the table and sat down on the lounge chair across from him.

"You doing okay?" he questioned, taking a sip of coffee.

"I'm doing better now." I nodded. I didn't want to tell him the truth. I didn't want to tell him that I was terrified and falling apart inside.

"Do you think it was him?"

I looked up into his eyes and hesitated before answering him. "I don't know? Maybe?"

"Then you think there is a possibility?"

I shrugged and wrapped my arms around myself. The breeze coming off the bay was cool, but with the increase of stress and anxiety I was going through, I was freezing. I didn't know what Dean was capable of. I had never pushed him this far.

"Are you cold? Want to sit over here with me?" he asked, patting the cushion between his legs.

"I'm okay. The coffee will warm me up." There was nothing I wanted more than to curl up with him on that chair and feel how warm and strong he was. I wanted to know what it would feel like to be in his arms again. I could feel him watching me, and I hoped that the look on my face didn't give away what I was thinking or feeling at that moment.

"So, when did you want to tell me the truth about what has gone on?" Parker looked me directly in the eye. "I know you haven't been completely honest with Elliott," he challenged.

"Of course, I was. I told Elliott the truth," I lied.

"Tatum, I know you, and so does Elliott. He isn't stupid. I know you're hiding something else. What about the bruises on your arms? You didn't tell him about those. Where did those come from?" The intense look he was giving me was making me uncomfortable.

"Parker..."

"Just know you can talk to me. It's me. I hope you'll feel comfortable enough to share with me when you're ready."

Holding my mug, I wrapped my hands around it, letting the heat soak into them while the rest of me shivered. I sat back and rested my head against the chair, wanting to tell him everything. Not just about the attack the night before I moved down, but everything. How I wished that maybe one day we could have another chance together. But I couldn't bring myself to say those words. I was afraid of what he would think of me, and I didn't want him to judge me. I'd given him a glimpse of it all the other day. Instead, I nodded, letting him know that one day, I would talk to him. For the next hour, we sat together and shared memories of our past.

After a while, he grew quiet. The night air and sounds of the water had relaxed me to the point I was having a hard time keeping my eyes open.

"Well, it's almost one. I'm going to take off and let you get some sleep." Parker checked his watch before standing up and grabbed our mugs to take inside.

I followed him in, locked the door, and pulled the curtain closed. He stood at the front door and wrapped his arms around me, giving me another of his amazing hugs. He was about to walk out the door when I grabbed his forearm.

Pausing, he turned and looked at me. "What is it, Tatum?"

"Parker..." His name felt good on my tongue. I swallowed hard as I looked from his eyes to his lips and back again. I didn't know how to ask him, so I blurted, "I don't want to be alone tonight. Will you...will you stay here with me?"

Parker went silent, looked away, and then back to me and took in a deep breath. I couldn't read the look on his face. "Give me a minute. I have to grab my gym bag from the back of my truck."

*P*ARKER

HOW COULD I SAY NO TO HER? AS I STOOD ON THAT porch, her eyes pleading with me, a gnawing feeling in my gut told me to stay. This was going to be a mistake, but how could I turn her down? She needed me.

"Let me grab my bag from the truck. I just finished at the gym when you called. I'd like to have a shower if that's okay."

Running down the front steps, I went to retrieve my

bag. Walking back toward the house, I couldn't help but check Tatum out. Her breasts looked perfect in the white tank top she wore, and I could see her nipples peeking through the fabric.

The tightness in my pants told me I was in trouble. I wished at that moment that Elliott was home and could stay with her instead, but I had promised him I would look out for her while he was gone.

I walked in, locking the door behind me, and shut off the outside light. Tatum brushed past me, close enough that her coconut body lotion invaded my nostrils. God, I loved that smell.

The bulge in my pants was getting painful. If I didn't take care of it in the shower, I was going to bust.

Tatum got me a towel from the closet and cleaned up some of her stuff in the bathroom.

"Everything good?"

I nodded, and after I shut the door, I turned the water on to let it warm up. A soft knock came on the door. "I left you a blanket and pillow on the couch," I heard Tatum call through the door.

I breathed in a sigh of relief. I was afraid we would have to share her bed. Even though I would have loved to do that, I wasn't sure I'd be able to.

"Thanks!" I yelled back. Climbing into the shower, I let the warm water fall over me. The heat felt great on my body. Closing my eyes, I imagined what it would feel like to have her lips wrapped around my cock, sucking slowly. I was throbbing and aching, so I reached down and took my cock in my hand and started stroking to that thought. It didn't take long for me to come, and once I had, I showered and got dried off. I didn't want her to wonder what was taking me so long.

Reaching into my gym bag, I realized all I had were my boxers to sleep in. Tatum would be in bed anyway, and besides, all she'd get was a show. All the hours in the gym had done my body good. I had nothing to be ashamed of and nothing she wouldn't like. I had caught her checking me out many times already.

I opened the bathroom door in time to see her cute ass walking into her bedroom. Her toned legs and her perfect, rounded ass looked amazing in the little shorts she was wearing. I could see the cheeks of her ass peeking out at the bottom of them.

She paused and turned, taking me all in, her eyes going from my shoulders to my chest down to my abs, stopping on my cock which was semi-hard after focusing my gaze on her. When she met my eyes her pupils were dilated, her lips parted, and she looked as if she had been caught doing something she shouldn't.

"Goodnight, Tatum." I gave her a wink and a soft smile.

I watched her bite her bottom lip as her eyes traveled back up to my face, a slight pink blush rising into her cheeks. "Night," she whispered and shut the door to her room, leaving it open a crack.

I grabbed the pillow off the back of the couch and put it to one end and sat down. This wasn't going to be comfortable. There was no way my six-foot frame was going to fit on her love seat. Sitting back, I put my feet up on the table and tried to relax.

A half hour later, my mind was still going to thoughts of those little white shorts. I kept trying to ignore the fact that she was lying in a bed on the other side of the wall. I needed to get my mind off her.

I checked my phone for any messages or emails, but there was nothing. I finally shut the light off, laid down, and stretched out, trying to relax. Another hour had passed by, and I was still wide awake. Sitting up, I turned on the light and was about to turn on the TV to see what was on, but instead, I somehow built up enough courage to go and knock lightly on her door.

"You still awake?" I whispered. It was only a moment before the light turned on in her bedroom. I pushed the door open and poked my head in.

"Something wrong?" she questioned as she sat up.

"No. It's a little tight out there on space is all. I needed to stretch, and I couldn't sleep." I walked into her room and propped her extra pillow up against the headboard and sat on the edge of the bed.

Her cheeks turning pink, she stood up out of bed as if I had burned her. "Oh my, I never thought about that. We can switch if you want? I didn't think about how tall you were."

I shook my head. "No, don't be silly, I've slept in worse spots. It's all good. You need a good night's sleep. I wanted to make sure you were okay." I patted the bed, gesturing for her to crawl back in.

Sitting back down, she covered up those beautiful legs of hers and looked down at her hands.

"Are you okay?" I hated to press her, but I was

following my gut—she needed to talk. Watching, I was pretty sure I noticed a tear fall down her cheek. "Tatum, look at me."

She wouldn't lift her head. She just kept looking at her hands.

I leaned over and placed my hand under her chin. Her skin was so soft. I lifted her face up to mine, and what I saw nearly broke me. Her eyes were filled with tears. I moved toward her and pulled her into my lap with ease and let her cry. The longer I held her, the calmer she became, until finally, she was quiet.

"My God, Parker, I'm so embarrassed. I really am fine," she said, sitting up and wiping the last of the stray tears away.

There was no way she was going to pull that shit with me again. She wasn't fine, and it was about time I found out exactly what had happened. "What happened, Tatum?"

She climbed out of my lap, laid down, and rolled onto her side, her back facing me. She was quiet for a while. "You have to promise not to tell Elliott. I'm not sure what he would do if he found out."

I wasn't sure I wanted to hear this, and she was putting me in a bad position: lie to my brother in blue and my best friend.

"Promise me, Parker." Her voice was soft.

I knew the only way I would ever find out was to promise. "I promise." I waited for her to roll over to face me, but she didn't. She took a deep breath, her shoulders shaking. She was crying again. I longed to reach out and hold her, but I waited.

"It has to do with those bruises that you asked me about." Her voice was low.

I could feel every muscle in my body clench. There was nothing I hated more than shitty guys who put their hands on a woman, but this one took the cake. He had put his hands on *her*. "I'm listening."

"It was after the night he spent at my place and I caught on to the fact he was still cheating on me. I hired a company to pack up my stuff, and I stayed with Jen up until the day the movers came. I felt I had imposed enough on her. I decided I was going to stay in a hotel at the airport until my flight left on Saturday. Well, Thursday night after the movers left, I headed to the hotel. I was exhausted. I fell asleep, and I woke to someone knocking on the door. I figured it was Jen coming to hang out, so I got up and opened the door. It was him. He forced his way in and assaulted me." Her body continued to shake from crying. "Please don't hate me, Parker, but Dean has hit me from day one. I'm sorry I lied to you and Elliott. I wouldn't blame you if you wanted to leave, I'll understand," she sobbed.

How could she think that? I hated to see her feeling this low and beat down. The guy had done a number on her; he had reduced her to a point where she felt completely worthless. I wasn't going to leave her or desert her. Instead, I moved closer to her, placing one arm under her head, and wrapped my other arm around her waist, pulling her tightly against my body.

"I'm not going anywhere, baby. I'm here now. You're safe with me. I am so sorry you've gone through all this."

She cried in my arms until she either felt safe or had become exhausted enough to fall asleep. Anger boiled inside me as I held her sleeping form. I was angry at the ass who treated her as if she didn't matter. But more so, I was angry at myself. If only I had tried harder to get her to stay with me all those years ago. For not showing her how important she was to me and putting my job ahead of her. Also, I was angry at the fact that I knew if I ever set my eyes on the guy, he'd be dead. Elliott wasn't the only one she had to worry about.

Chapter Thirteen

Tatum

I OPENED MY EYES AND LOOKED AROUND THE ROOM. THE sun was just peeking through the curtains when I saw a hand sticking out from under my pillow. I could feel the slow and steady puff of his breath against my neck just before I was pulled back against Parker's chest, and I could feel his hardness pressing into me. I was so warm and comfortable lying in his arms. It had been the best night's sleep I'd had since moving to Emerald Bay. I waited a few more minutes before I moved, to be sure he was still asleep. Then I gently lifted his arm from around my waist and climbed out of bed, being careful not to wake him.

I stood on the back deck looking out over the bay. The morning sunlight bounced off the colored leaves, making them even brighter. I couldn't help but wonder what

Parker thought of me. Years ago, I never would have stood to be treated the way I had been treated by Dean, but somehow, I grew to accept it. I was disappointed with myself, and I was glad I couldn't see the look on his face last night when I told him. I didn't want to see the disappointment or disgust in his eyes. I had already seen enough the night I told Elliott. Those thoughts kept playing over and over in my head, driving me crazy and making me uneasy. I remembered how Elliott had urged me to call Parker after we broke up. He had the same look of disgust and pity on his face then as he did the other night.

I walked into the apartment I shared with my brother and went straight to my bedroom. It had been a long day at work. I was tired, and I missed Parker something terrible. I wanted so badly to call him. I closed my bedroom door and flopped down on my bed. I lay with my arm over my eyes, listening to silence. My bedroom door creaked open, and Elliott stood inside the doorway staring at me.

"What are you doing?"

"Trying to relax and calm my mind. What's up, Elliott?" Truth was, I was just plain miserable. It had been six months since Parker left, and I missed him more than ever.

"I talked to Parker today. Why don't you pick up that phone and call him?"

"He doesn't want to hear from me, Elliott."

"Really? How would you know? You haven't spoken to him in months, Tatum."

I could tell he was getting impatient with me. After all, I had been driving him crazy. Should I call? Shouldn't I call?

"Why would he want to hear from me? I was horrible to him. I didn't trust him."

"I don't think that's the case, Tatum. With everything that happened, you couldn't take another major change. Even though he didn't want to go without you, he understood. I think you owe it to yourself to call him."

I rolled over onto my stomach. Why was Elliott always right?

"He didn't understand. He left."

"Yes, he left, you're right. He couldn't turn down that job. Give the guy a break, Tatum. Just because he went, doesn't mean he didn't understand what you were going through or that he didn't love you. I'm the one who's been talking to him for the past six months. He misses you."

"If he misses me so much then why doesn't he call me?"

"You're being unreasonable, Tatum. Do you miss him? Because almost every conversation we have with each other either begins or ends with his name."

I was being unreasonable, and I knew it. Did I miss him? What a stupid question. I missed everything about that man.

"Yes," I cried.

Elliott walked forward and threw a piece of paper on my bed then returned to the door. "Do yourself a favor and call him." He pulled the door shut.

I picked the piece of paper up off the bed and looked at the phone number Elliott had scrawled out. Rolling onto my side, I grabbed my cell phone and stared at the number written on the paper. My stomach began knotting up as my finger hovered over the call button.

I couldn't bring myself to do it. I was ashamed of how I'd treated him when we broke up. He deserved better than me.

The sound of the door opening jarred me out of my memory. I glanced over my shoulder to see Parker step outside. My gaze traveled from his broad, bare shoulders and hard chest to his rock-hard abs, right down to the deep-carved V peeking out of his boxers. I turned my head and rested my chin on my hand. I wasn't ready to face him this morning. At least, not yet.

He came up behind me and rubbed my arms with his strong hands. "Morning, beautiful."

"Morning." I stood up, his arms wrapping around me from behind. He pulled me into his chest. "I hope I didn't wake you?"

"Nope."

"I have coffee on. I'll get you a cup." I hurried away, but he grabbed a hold of me before I could get too far, pulling me into him again.

"There's no rush," he said, finding my eyes.

I pulled out of his grasp, avoiding his gaze, walked to the other side of the deck, and stood fidgeting with the tie on my robe. "I just figured you would want to get going. I mean, I'm sure you have things you need to get done before you go to work today." I felt uneasy. I didn't want him to feel obligated to stay with me. I had, after all, sprung it on him to stay last night.

He walked to me and placed his hand over top of mine, shaking the tie from my grasp. "Tatum... What's wrong?"

"Nothing. It's nothing," I said, looking down at the deck floor.

He placed his finger under my chin and raised my head to look at him. His gaze moving from my eyes to my mouth, he leaned in and brushed my lips with his. Heat curled down my spine and pooled between my legs. Placing one hand on the side of my face, he pulled me into him with the other, deepening the kiss, his tongue finding mine. I could feel his protection in his kiss.

When he pulled back to look at me, his blue eyes danced in the sunlight. "I'm not going anywhere, baby. I'm here for you. You don't need to be afraid of me leaving or not wanting to be with you."

It was as if he had read my mind. It was as if a weight had been lifted from my shoulders the moment he said those words.

Chapter Fourteen

Dean

I sat at my desk, impatiently waiting for the call. What the fuck was the matter with this guy? He knew he was on a deadline, and now he was late. Being late pissed me off more than anything. I had employed this man to find Tatum, and he was being paid well. I fumbled through the stack of papers in front of me when my phone finally rang. Picking it up, I put the receiver to my ear.

"I've done as you instructed. It's her," the voice said over the phone.

"Are you sure? Did you actually see her?"

"Yes, I saw her. It's her."

"Did she see you?"

"No, sir." The line went quiet. I could hear him clear

his throat on the other end. He was nervous, and so he should be. "There's something else."

"What is it?"

"You're not going to like what I have to tell you."

"What is it?" I demanded.

"She called someone. He showed up and walked the perimeter of the house."

"Was it her brother? The guy I showed you?"

"No, sir."

I clenched my teeth so hard I thought they were going to crack. "How long was he there for?"

"He spent the night."

"*Fuck*." I slammed the phone down and smashed my fist on my desk. Rage swept over me. Who the fuck thought he had the right? She was *mine*!

Chapter Fifteen

Tatum

Jen arrived early Saturday morning. I had missed her something terrible. Our only conversations took place on the phone, and that wasn't the same as hanging out and talking in person. When Elliott and Parker found out she was coming for a visit, they insisted on taking us out for the day. We'd be spending the day on Parker's boat, followed by a bonfire on the beach. After I picked her up from the airport, we headed to the mall to shop for some outfits. We had planned just to hang out and watch movies, which required nothing fancy, but the boys had different ideas. It had been years since the four of us hung out. It was sure to be a blast.

Jen and I started getting ready as soon as we got back to my place. The boys would be picking us up in about an hour. I changed into the skimpy black bikini that Jen insisted I buy. In her words, it accentuated my breasts, and Parker would like that. I brushed my hair and threw it into a ponytail before clipping it up. I put my white lace cover-up over the bathing suit and added a change of clothes to my beach bag for this evening.

"Are you almost ready?" I yelled to Jen who had taken over my bathroom.

She walked out of the bathroom in her cover-up which I noticed hid way more than mine did. Come to think of it, so did the bathing suit. She handed me the two beach towels we bought and her change of clothes to put in my bag.

"Yep, I'm ready. You look amazing!" she said, checking me out.

"Yeah, well, I may look amazing, but I feel very naked." I pulled on my little white cotton shorts to wear until we hit the boat.

"I can't wait to check out Parker and see how he's grown." I rolled my eyes at Jen. She wasn't going to let this go. "I'm sure he is as unbelievably hot as he was in college."

"Good, you check him out." I stuck my tongue out at her and she laughed. I was beginning to regret telling her anything that had happened between us. I headed into the kitchen to make us a quick snack.

"Oh please, admit for once that you want him."

I was quiet. I couldn't even begin to forget that kiss. I could still vividly feel his lips on mine, his hand on my cheek. I did want him more than she knew, but I wasn't ready to admit it.

"So, have you heard from that ass back home?" I could see the seriousness in Jen's eyes.

"Unfortunately, yes, he has called—on my new number. Not too sure how he got it, but I haven't heard from him since then."

"Have you told Elliott anything?"

"I did. He wasn't too happy, but he does know now. You were right, I should have told him from the start." I handed her a sandwich and sat down at the table.

"I'm glad you told him."

I cut her off before she could say anything else. "All right, enough of this conversation. Let's just have a good time, okay." Sitting down, I checked my phone for any messages from Elliott or Parker. There was nothing from them, but sure enough, Dean had left one.

DEAN: I'M COMING FOR YOU.

I felt the color drain from my face. Getting up from the table, I started busying myself around the kitchen. I could feel myself starting to hyperventilate and knew I needed to calm my breathing.

"Everything okay?" Jen asked, taking a bite of her sandwich.

The room was starting to spin, and I could feel myself getting light-headed.

"Tatum?"

Grabbing hold of the counter, I steadied myself. "Yes, everything is fine." I barely recognized my own voice. I was scared, but I certainly didn't want her to know he had messaged me. I wanted to have a good time today. Looking out the front window, I saw Elliott and Parker walking up the walkway. "Boys are here."

"Ladies!" Elliott's voice boomed as he pushed his way through the door. "Let's get going!" He gave Jen a great big hug.

I'd always thought they would make a great couple. Jen had had a crush on him forever, but Elliott always told me he wasn't interested in his younger sister's friend. Parker came in behind Elliott and met my gaze. I followed his eyes as they skimmed down my body then traveled back up. He noticed me watching him and gave me a small smile. I loved that smile.

"Hey, sis! Do you have anything to go today?"

I pointed to the bag on the floor by the door. "Oh, and the cooler out front. It's filled with some drinks."

Elliott grabbed the bag and Parker the cooler, and they went to put them in the back of his truck.

I turned to grab my phone and decided against it. The last thing I wanted was for that idiot to have access to me today, so I shut the phone off and left it on the table. As we walked out the front door, Jen tapped me on the shoulder.

"You failed to mention how *hot* he turned out to be."

"We ended a long time ago, Jen," I said, pulling the front door closed and locking it.

"Not Parker. I mean he's hot, and you should totally go for him—I even saw him check you out—but I was talking about Elliott."

IT WAS A COOL NIGHT AND CLOUDS WERE STARTING TO blow in over the water. The boat had been docked and we had found a spot on the beach for the bonfire. Jen and I were waiting on the beach for the guys to bring over the wood from Parker's truck.

"So, you and Elliott spent a lot of time together today?"

"Yeah we found a great little reef with a ton of fish. It was amazing. We snorkeled around, and then we took a break out on the sand bar, soaking up some rays." She smiled. "You guys looked rather cozy when we got back to the boat." She nudged my shoulder, giving me that knowing look.

"We were sharing a chair."

"Looked like it was a little more than that, if you ask me." She laughed. She had been doing this to me all day, every time she caught us together.

"I was getting burned. He put sunscreen on my back. I mean, what choice did I have? You left me high and dry to hang with my brother."

"Whatever. I'm sure it wasn't that bad." Jen looked off in the distance. "Here come the guys now."

Both Elliott and Parker had an armful of wood, and each of them carried a blanket for us to sit on. It didn't take them long to get the fire going, as Jen and I spread the blankets out. Elliott sat down behind Jen and pulled her between his legs, letting her rest against him. He kept whispering in her ear, making her giggle, which I found endearing. I watched them while Parker threw more logs onto the fire. After, he sat down behind me, mimicking Elliott and Jen, and I relaxed against him.

Jen looked across at me and smiled. I watched as she whispered something into Elliott's ear, and then elbowing him in the ribs, she stood up and brushed herself off. "We're going to go for a walk down the beach." Jen took hold of Elliott's hand and pulled him up off the blanket. Parker and I watched as they walked off into the darkness.

"They look like they're getting along well," Parker whispered into my ear. "Do you think they'll get together?" His breath tickled my neck as he spoke, and I could feel goose bumps forming.

"Maybe, but he better not hurt her. She's been crushing on him since college, even though she won't admit it."

"It's okay."

"How can you say that?"

"Because so has he," Parker whispered again, his breath dancing along my skin. "And I know someone who's crushing on you."

I closed my eyes and welcomed the surge of warmth that ran through my body. He wrapped his arms around me and kissed my neck. "You looked super sexy today."

I didn't know how to respond to that. It had been a long time since someone thought I looked sexy. I looked down the beach in the direction Elliott and Jen had gone, but couldn't see them. Turning, I looked at Parker. As he stared into my eyes, I realized, I hadn't stopped loving him all this time. Events had separated us, but he was right, we would find our way back together. Maybe we were.

Leaning forward, he placed his mouth on mine, his tongue coaxing my lips apart for a deep kiss. I felt like I was on fire. Warmth pooled between my legs. His hand found its way into my hair while he sucked on my bottom lip and his tongue explored my mouth.

I turned between his legs and got on my knees. He placed both hands beneath my butt, lifting me so I was straddling his lap. We continued kissing, his hands exploring my body. I could feel his hardness through his shorts, and I ground down on him so he was rubbing me in just the right spot.

"Are you wet for me?" he whispered into my mouth.

I could feel the heat rise to my face. I leaned back and looked him in the eyes. Taking his hand, I placed the drawstring of my shorts between his fingers, giving him permission to find out. A tiny groan escaped his throat. He hesitated at first, then he pulled the string, kissing me as he went. His touch sent little electric shocks through me. He placed his hand on my belly, prepared to slide it inside my shorts, but suddenly, he stilled. We could hear laughter getting closer. I jumped off his lap and sat beside him as he adjusted himself in time for Elliott and Jen to appear out of the darkness.

"Hey, Parker, you mind giving Tatum a ride home? Jen and I are going to take off," he said, his arm around Jen.

I looked to Jen and she smiled back at me.

"Yeah, I don't mind. Do you mind?" he asked, looking to me.

"No, I don't mind."

As soon as Jen and Elliott were gone, Parker grabbed me and laid me back on the blanket. Propping himself up on his elbow, he looked down into my eyes. The air grew thick while he studied my face. Leaning down he placed his mouth over mine, moving down to my neck and back up to my mouth.

"Where were we?" he whispered, kissing me deeper, his hands traveling back to my waist. His fingers tickled as they ran along my tummy and the waistband of my shorts. He looked down into my face. I could see the desire in his eyes as he slid his hand down my shorts. I spread my legs just enough to feel his fingers slide over top of my wet panties.

"Fuck you're so wet," he whispered into my mouth as he kissed me again.

I let out a moan as his fingers brushed over my clit. He trailed kisses to my earlobe.

"Touch me," he moaned as he sucked my earlobe into his mouth, and then ran his teeth over it. "Feel what you're doing to me."

I froze, Dean's face suddenly flashing through my mind, and my thoughts went to the night at my apartment. I reached up and placed both my hands onto Parkers chest, stopping him.

"Please stop," I pleaded.

He instantly pulled his hand from my shorts and sat up and raked his fingers through his hair. I could see the hurt in his eyes. "What's wrong? What did I do?"

"I can't do this." I wasn't ready for this. The bite and those words were exactly what Dean loved to use.

Parker sat up and looked toward the water for a few minutes. He said nothing more, even though I could see he had a thousand thoughts running through his mind. He stood up and piled sand onto the fire to smother it, while I picked up and folded the blankets. He grabbed the pile of blankets out of my hand, and we walked in silence to his truck. He didn't bother opening my door for me. Instead, he got into the truck and started it up.

I had blown it with him. Memories quickly flooded back to the night he walked out of my life without so much as a word. A lump formed in my throat. I wished I could tell him what happened that made me want to stop. It wasn't him, but rather the memories I held onto.

The drive back to my place seemed to take forever, and I was afraid to look over at him. I kept my eyes focused on the dark houses as we passed by them, tears filling my eyes. Why couldn't things have gone differently? Why did I have to open my mouth? Why couldn't I have closed my eyes and shoved Dean out of my mind?

When we pulled up outside my house, he put the truck in park but still said nothing.

"Did you want to come in?" I asked.

"Not tonight. I don't think it would be a good idea."

I turned my head and looked at him before I got out of the truck. He didn't even turn to look at me, instead keeping his eyes straight ahead, his jaw set. I could see the rejection and hurt all over his face.

Opening the door, I got out of the truck and shut the door. Normally, he would wait until I was inside before he drove away, but not this time. As soon as my feet touched the pavement and the door was shut, he said goodnight and reversed out of the driveway. There was no stopping the ache in my throat or the sting in my eyes—the tears started to pour.

I walked up the front steps, wiping at my eyes so I could see to put the key in the lock. I hadn't left the outside light on and fumbled with the key. After a couple seconds, I walked in, shutting the door and locking it behind me. I turned the light on over the kitchen sink and put the kettle on. I wouldn't get any sleep tonight, but I went to get changed anyway.

"It's about fucking time you were home!"

I heard that gruff voice as soon as I flicked the light on in my bedroom. My chest rose and fell rapidly. I froze. I didn't even need to turn around to know who it belonged to.

"What are you doing here?" My chest tightened with fear as I turned to face him.

"You should be more careful about locking doors, Tatum. Anyone could get in here." He spoke calmly as he sauntered toward me, his eyes skimming over my barely covered body. He reached out and ran his finger down my cheek. "I told you I was coming to get you, and it looks like I'm just in time. I guess I need to teach you a lesson, since you're running around, acting like some slut with that asshole." His eyes skimmed down my body. "You look like a fucking tramp in that outfit."

He grabbed hold of my hair and pulled my head back, forcing me to look him in the eyes. I could feel bile rise into my throat.

"You're mine. What are you thinking?" he sneered.

He let go of my hair. I tried to shove him away, so I could run, but instead he grabbed both of my arms tight in his hands and threw me onto the bed. "No, you're not getting away that easy again, you bitch," he hissed. Crawling on top of me, his knees locked my hands at my side. He grabbed at my cover-up, ripping it and the bathing suit top off me. "Dress like a whore, be treated like one," he said. Leaning in, he whispered into my ear, "I'll fuck you like one too."

He leaned down to bite and suck on my nipples, and my stomach threatened to release its contents. The room started getting smaller and darker. I fought for every breath, feeling as if I would pass out.

A pounding on the front door rang through the house like a gunshot. I tried to scream, but Dean covered my mouth with his hand.

I wiggled under him, trying hard to get away, but with his hand over my mouth and the lack of oxygen, I tired quickly.

The pounding continued. "Tatum, it's me, open up!" I heard Parker shout.

Dean stilled. "Is that the asshole?"

I tried hard to shout through my covered mouth, but it was no good. I heard Parker bang on the door again and call my name one more time before everything went silent. All I could hear was my heart pounding in my ears, and I felt as if I could faint.

Dean looked down at me. "No one is coming to save you. Now, I'm going to remove my hand from your mouth. I don't want to hear a fucking thing out of you. If I do, I promise you will regret it."

He slowly released his hand from my mouth, and I felt him get off the bed. He grabbed me under the knees and pulled me down to the edge of the bed and forced his body between my thighs. Crying, I felt his hand slide my bathing suit bottom to the side. He was about to undo his zipper when the sound of heavy footsteps came charging into the room.

"Get the fuck off her!"

Dean released his hold on me at the sound of Parker's voice, and I quickly sat up, trying to cover myself. I watched as Parker grabbed him by shoulder and punched him in the stomach. Dean doubled over, and Parker forced him down to the ground. He pulled a pair of cuffs from his back pocket and cuffed his hands, and then grabbed another pair for his feet. He stood towering over him.

Parker looked to me and grabbed the blanket off the bottom of the bed and wrapped it around my shaking body. He picked me up and took me out to the couch and sat me down. Tears poured down my face. Thank God, he had come back.

He went back into the bedroom and came out with some clothes for me then shut the bedroom door, leaving Dean on the floor. Sitting down beside me, he pulled me onto his lap and pulled me into his strong, protective embrace. I began to relax into his body, and off in the distance, I heard sirens blaring.

Chapter Sixteen

Tatum

DEAN HAD BEEN ARRESTED. PARKER HAD TRIED TO CALL
Elliott and Jen on the way to the station but couldn't get an
answer. I sat in a quiet room in the police station wrapped
in the blanket from Parker's truck. One of the female offi-
cers had gotten me a hot cup of tea, but it had done little
to warm me up. I had already spoken to the sergeant, and I
was now waiting for Parker to finish up with him.

I sat there, my hands wrapped around the paper cup,
trying to gather and hold any heat I could. I leaned my
head back against the wall and closed my eyes. The door
creaked open, causing me to jump. Parker walked in and
took a seat across from me. He placed his hands on my
thighs.

"Are you going to be okay?"

I looked down at the floor to hide my face from him. It was easier to lie to him that way. I shook my head yes and took another sip of the hot tea.

"Harrison." The sergeant poked his head in the door. "You can take Tatum home now. If we need anything else, we'll call."

I looked to Parker. I was too terrified of being alone in my house after all of this. He held out his hand to me, and I reached out to grasp it. I stood up as he wrapped his arm around my waist and pulled me into him, walking me slowly out of the room.

"He can't get out, can he?" Panic arose in my chest.

"Well, not right now. He'll need to see a judge before bail can be set. No worries. We will be notified if the time comes that he is released," Parker spoke in a hushed voice.

"But if he gets out, he will find me, Parker. He will come for me."

He pulled me into him tighter and urged me forward with his hand on the small of my back. "Let's not worry about that right now, Tatum. We are going to get home and get some rest."

"Parker, I don't want to go home."

"Baby, you're coming home with me. I won't let anything happen to you."

"Harrison, if she needs help with this, you let us know. I have explained to her there is counseling that we can arrange for her."

Parker nodded and guided me out the station door. We were walking down the front steps when we heard our names being called and turned to see Elliott and Jen rushing over.

Elliott grabbed me and wrapped his arms around me. "My God, Tatum, are you okay?"

I nodded, hugging him back. I could feel that familiar burn in my eyes but refused to give in to the tears.

As soon as Elliott let me go, Jen stepped in to hug me. "I should have come back with you. This wouldn't have happened."

"No, it could have been worse. It's okay. I'm fine. It's late, guys. I just want to get some sleep." I didn't want them to make a big deal over this.

"Well, I'm going to come home with you. I don't want you to be alone," Jen finished, looking to Elliott.

"The house is still under evidence review," Parker reminded her.

"You can come back to my place, stay with Jen and I. Parker, you as well if you want," Elliott said, nodding at Jen.

Shaking my head, I looked to all of them. "Guys, it's all right. You both go back to whatever you were doing. I'm okay. Parker can take me home. It's all good. No need to make a fuss over me," I insisted.

They all looked at me, almost analyzing me to make sure I was telling them the truth. It was suffocating as their eyes penetrated my very being. I opened Parker's truck door and climbed up, pulling the door shut behind me, and closed my eyes.

When Parker didn't immediately get in the truck, I opened my eyes and watched as they congregated on the sidewalk. Every once in a while, Jen and Elliott would glance over their shoulders to look at me. They could talk about me all they wanted. I would be fine.

PARKER

"WHAT THE HELL HAPPENED?" ELLIOTT QUESTIONED.

How was I going to explain to him what had gone down? He would be pissed to know I left her outside and took off. It wasn't like me, but I couldn't help it. I was hurt and needed to distance myself. Looking at both him and Jen, I swallowed hard.

"You're going to be pissed with me, Elliott. It probably wouldn't have happened if I wasn't being an ass."

"What are you talking about, Parker?"

"We left the beach; things kind of got a little hot between us. She suddenly wanted to leave. So we packed up, I dropped her off, and I left before she was inside."

Elliott glared at me. I could feel the heat coming from his eyes. He had trusted me with his sister, and I had disappointed him and her. I wasn't proud of myself.

"Anyways, I got to my driveway, and something in my gut told me to go back. I tried to shake it but couldn't. I ran in the house and grabbed my gun and two sets of cuffs from my bag before going back. When I pulled into the driveway, I saw the light on in the kitchen. I watched as her bedroom light then went on, and I sat debating what I was going to say to her when she opened the door.

"I got out of the truck and walked up and knocked on the door. I thought it strange that she didn't answer, so I called her name and still nothing. I thought I may be scaring her, so I told her it was me and still nothing. When I went to leave, I heard what sounded like a call for help.

"I called nine-one-one, and then I went around to the back of the house and found the back slider to the living room open. When I stepped in, that's when I heard him talking to her. I'm not going to tell you all the details because I'm sure you can read all that in the police report, but it wasn't pretty."

Elliott finally unclenched his fists and started to relax.

"I'm sorry that I didn't go in with her, Elliott."

Jen rubbed Elliott's back and wiped the tears from her eyes.

He stood, taking me in. "The main thing is you got to her before anything worse happened, and for that I am thankful. I just hope she's going to be okay." He peaked around to look at Tatum.

I turned and looked over my shoulder at her. She sat wrapped in the blanket with her head back and her eyes closed. I silently prayed for that too.

"Do me a favor, Parker?"

"Anything."

"Can you take her to your place?"

"You've got it. You guys get home and get some rest. We can meet up tomorrow. Once again, Elliott, I am sorry."

Elliott wrapped his arm around Jen's waist and led her to his truck. "It's okay, Parker. Call if you need anything!" he shouted over his shoulder.

"You know it." I walked around and climbed up into the truck and pulled away from the curb.

Chapter Seventeen

Parker

I was so fucking mad; I needed something to calm my nerves. I wanted to kill that fucker for touching my girl. I was still pissed with myself for being such an ass earlier. Thank God, Elliott didn't take a swing at me.

I sat on the couch with my feet up on the coffee table, watching the news, trying hard to calm myself down. Tatum didn't need this right now. I heard a soft voice behind me and looked to see her watching me. My heart sped up at the sight of her.

"Come sit." I patted the spot beside me. "I made you a tea." I nodded to the cup on the table, swallowing the lump in my throat.

She walked over and sat down, picked the mug up, and

took a sip, closing her eyes as she recognized it was her favorite tea—chamomile.

"You remembered my favorite tea."

"I remember lots of things about you, Tatum. And besides, it's good tea. It helps me relax." I winked at her. She had told me that for years when we dated.

We sat in silence. She pulled her legs up to her chest and got comfortable in the corner of my couch, her head lazing on the backrest.

"What made you come back to the house tonight?" Her soft voice was barely audible as she asked me the question that I had prayed she wouldn't ask.

I muted the TV and turned to look at her.

"Well?" She sat waiting for me to answer. She looked so tiny curled up.

"Do you want the honest answer?"

She nodded her head and took another drink of tea.

"As I drove away, I began to feel awful. You turned me away, and I acted like a pissy little teenager. I didn't want you to think I was going anywhere. I wanted to let you know that it was okay to say no to me."

I looked away from her. "I thought it was odd when you didn't answer the door, considering I had just dropped you off. I also knew you hadn't gone to bed yet because I watched as you turned on the bedroom light. Just as I was going to walk away, something felt wrong, and I thought I heard you call for help. So, I went around the back of the house and saw the back door was open. I didn't want to scare you, so I listened, and then I heard him. You know the rest." I could feel the anger begin to course through me again.

She was silent again. I was afraid to look at her for fear she would see the vulnerability in my eyes. It took every fiber of my being not to kill him for what he had done to her. I couldn't let her see that in my face. The feelings I had for her were growing stronger by the day. I couldn't go down this path again just to have my feelings destroyed. I had lost her once, and I was afraid it would happen again. Only this time, I wasn't sure I would survive it.

Taking a deep breath, I took a drink of my tea and turned to her. One look and I could see tears filling her eyes, some rolling down her cheeks, the look hitting me in the pit of my stomach.

"I didn't turn you down because I didn't want you, Parker. I wanted you more in that moment than I ever have. Truth is that wanting never stopped, and being around you again, that wanting has just gotten stronger."

Her words caught me by surprise. It took all the courage I had, but I turned my head to look at her.

"Your words, your actions in that moment on the beach reminded me of him. That's why I stopped you. You should know that I'm so thankful that you cared enough to turn around and come back tonight, because if you hadn't of come when you did, I don't know what would have happened." She let out a loud, uncontrollable sob and started to shake.

I moved over to her, pulling her into me. Placing her head on my shoulder, I held her while she cried. "Cared enough, you never have to worry about that. I have never stopped caring about you. I want you to know that you're safe now. I've got you."

She cried harder, pushing herself closer to me. It broke my heart having her cry like this and made me angrier at the same time. The fucker was lucky he was behind bars tonight. My main priority sat in my arms; she was all that mattered.

Lifting her with ease onto my lap, I held her against my chest as tight as I could, at times fighting back my own tears. When she finally calmed and lifted her head to look at me, I placed my hand on the side of her face. Looking into her eyes, I brought my lips to hers and kissed her, soft and tender yet hard and forceful, with everything I had in me to give. I put my arms under her legs, picked her up, and carried her to my bedroom, her head resting on my chest.

I had already turned the bed down, so I laid her gently onto the mattress. Taking the blanket, I pulled it up over her body. I placed a kiss on her forehead. "Get some sleep, baby."

I shut the light off and grabbed a pair of boxers from my dresser on my way out of the room. Pulling the door shut part way, I went to walk down the hall when I heard her call my name. "What is it?" I asked, turning back.

"Where are you going?" I could see her faintly in the light that spilled into the room.

"Just going to jump in the shower. I'll be on the couch if you need anything," I said, turning around again.

"Please, I don't want to be alone tonight." I heard a sob

escape her throat. I didn't know what to say. I wasn't sure I could do this. "Please, Parker."

"Okay, give me a few minutes to shower." I walked down to the living room and shut the TV off and headed to the bathroom. Turning the water on, I climbed into a hot shower and tried to let my feelings wash away.

TATUM

PARKER WALKED DOWN THE HALL. I HEARD THE TV GO off and the water in the shower start running. I was glad he said he would spend the night beside me. I closed my eyes and thought of the beach, how safe I felt in Parker's arms, and how good it felt to be kissed by him again. I remembered how it felt to have him touch me. I could feel myself getting aroused at the thought. I wanted him to make me feel the way I was supposed to feel, not like the dirty waste that Dean had made me think I was—the dirty waste I felt I was. I wanted him.

I pulled the blankets up to my nose and inhaled; his scent was intoxicating. I could feel that familiar ache between my legs from earlier that evening. I was just about to slip my hand in between my legs when I heard the water stop.

Rolling onto my side with my back to the door, I waited with my eyes closed, my pulse hammering in my ears. I felt the bed sink when he sat on the edge, and then he crawled in, trying hard not to disturb me. When the bed stilled, I rolled onto my other side and propped myself up on my elbow and looked at him. He lay there with his hands tucked behind his head, the moonlight falling through the window onto his chest.

"Parker."

"Yes."

"I wanted to say I am sorry."

He looked over at me, his gaze meeting mine. "What for?"

"Everything," I answered weakly.

He rolled onto his side. "Listen, Tatum, don't go blaming yourself for what happened tonight."

I put my hand on his bicep to stop him and lay on my back. "I'm not talking about that," I said, staring up into his eyes.

"Then what is it?"

"I'm sorry that I watched you walk way. I wanted to call you, to come to you after you and tell you what a mistake I'd made."

"Why didn't you?"

"I didn't think you would want to hear from me."

He bent down and placed his lips on mine, kissing me hard. "How could you think that? Walking away from you was the hardest thing I've ever done. My God, Tatum, I was in love with you."

Tears escaped my eyes as he kissed me again, his hands running down the length of my body. They settled on my ass, and he pulled me into his body. I wrapped my leg over his hip, so he could pull me closer to him. It didn't take long for me to feel his arousal against me; he was so hard and seemed much bigger than earlier. As his hands ran back up my body, they grazed the side of my breast, causing a soft moan to escape from my throat.

"Make love to me, please," I moaned as he continued to kiss along my collarbone.

He stilled. "I'm not sure that's a good idea, Tatum." He looked from my eyes to my mouth and back again.

I lifted my head from my pillow and kissed him. "Please, show me what it's like to be loved." A single tear escaped my eye.

While holding me in his arms, he kissed me softly then took hold of the shirt I was wearing and lifted it over my head. I watched his eyes as they focused on my breasts and back up to my face. Kissing me deeply, his tongue explored my mouth. He moved down and took my nipple in his mouth, his tongue running circles around it. My back arched off the bed, heat pooling between my legs. I felt his hand trace circles on the inside of my thigh. He exhaled sharply as he ran his fingers through my wetness, rubbing my clit with slow, soft circles. A moan escaped my lips as I arched my back up into him, biting my bottom lip. He kissed his way down my body, stopping at my waist, and lingered there, placing light kisses over my abdomen. He placed his hands on the insides of my thighs and opened me, putting me on display for him.

"You're so wet." He slid both hands under my ass and lifted me up off the bed and kissed the insides of my thighs.

Another moan escaped my lips as he lapped at my

middle, my hands grasping the sheets. He continued to lick and suck my clit, bringing me closer and closer to orgasm.

I was about to go over the edge when he stopped and kissed the insides of my thighs again, and then I felt him get off the bed. His eyes were on me as he lowered his boxers and sprung free. My eyes wandered down his body to his cock, and my jaw dropped. He was much bigger than I thought, and so hard.

Kneeling back on the bed, he rubbed my clit and then slid one finger and then another into me, stretching me. He removed his fingers and while watching my face, he placed himself at my opening and slid himself slowly, inch by agonizing inch, into me, stretching me. A hard moan escaped his lips. Once he was seated inside, he stopped moving and let me adjust to him.

"Fuck, you are so tight. You feel amazing." He groaned into my mouth as he sucked my bottom lip.

I felt him flex his hips, and then he started moving inside of me. Every pump getting harder, deeper, than the previous. It wasn't long before I could feel myself start to go over the edge. Holding onto him, I buried my face into his shoulder to quiet my cries.

"That's it, baby."

The sound of his thick voice sent me over the edge, and I let myself go, clenching around him. He gave one final pump, and he, too, let go, filling me. He collapsed on top of me, his breathing hard and heavy.

He rolled off me and pulled me into his side, kissing me on the forehead. Closing my eyes, I fell into a deep sleep.

Chapter Eighteen

Tatum

PARKER AND I MET ELLIOTT AND JEN THE NEXT
morning at the airport. Jen's flight was leaving at noon, and
this was the last chance I would get to spend with her until
her next visit. We walked into the airport, and I spotted
Jen and Elliott at the coffee bar right away. I took a seat
beside Jen while Parker went to the counter to join Elliott
and grab our drinks.

Her expression turned serious the moment I sat down.
"I'm glad you are okay." She wrapped her arms around me,
hugging me.

I hugged her back. "I'm good. You don't need to
worry."

"Sooo, how did your night go?"

I smiled back, giving her a knowing look.

"You didn't?"

I could feel myself blush.

"Oh my God, you did!"

I nodded, feeling the room get hot. "We did. I know I don't need to ask you though," I said, laughing.

"Nope, never been one to hold back. I always go with the flow, you know that. You should have tried it a long time ago. It wouldn't have taken you guys so long to get together if you followed in my footsteps." She laughed, bumping into my shoulder. "Okay, so are you going to spill and tell me how it was?"

"I can't even begin to tell you, but it was nothing short of amazing. After last night, I wished he had been my first. Instead, I gave myself up to a cold, ruthless lover. A man who never took no for an answer." I hadn't been ready to share those feelings with anyone until now.

"Well, to be fair to yourself, at the time that happened, you didn't know what he would become. Go easy on yourself."

Looking up and noticing the guys were still in line, I looked to Jen. "And not like I want to know because he's my brother and all, so please spare me the details, but how was it for you?"

I watched Jen as she looked over to where they stood. I could tell that she was more in love with Elliott than I had ever seen her. "She smiled to herself and looked over at Elliott again. "I fear I'm in trouble with this one." She giggled.

I had never heard Jen say those words about anyone, nor had I ever seen the look on her face that presented itself to me at that moment. "I was afraid this would happen."

"He wants to date—exclusively," she said quietly and smiled at me.

Jen had never been exclusive with anyone. She always did whatever appealed to her. I was sure this was scaring the crap out of her.

"And?"

"I told him yes. He won't be able to visit often, but we will see how the next little while goes, and then we can decide. It's not like we don't know one another at all, so that makes it a little easier. Between you and me, I'd even be willing to move."

"Please take your time and make sure. It's not that I wouldn't love having you down here, but I want you to make sure this is what you want before you drop every-thing. For once, don't let spontaneity rule your life. You're not only dealing with your feelings here," I warned her.

I knew she wouldn't listen to me. It wasn't in her DNA. I loved her like a sister and didn't want to see either of them jump into something with their eyes closed.

A cup dropped down in front of me, and I felt warm hands on my shoulders. "Your coffee, my dear." Parker pulled the nearest chair up beside me and sat down, wrap-ping his arm around me.

We sat and talked until the first call for Jen's flight. I could tell she and Elliott wanted some time to be alone, so Parker and I said our good-byes early and headed home.

Chapter Nineteen

Tatum

I HAD SPENT THE LAST FOUR DAYS AT PARKER'S. THE police had finally called to let me know they had collected all the evidence they needed. I was welcome to return to my home. I wasn't looking forward to going back. I didn't want to say anything to Parker, though. After all, it had taken nearly two hours to convince him to take me home.

Pulling into the driveway, he shut the truck off. "Are you sure you're going to be okay alone here tonight while I'm at work? You can always stay at my place, if it makes you feel better."

"I know I can, but I will be okay." I had decided that this was something I had to do. I didn't want to get involved in this conversation again. I couldn't stay at Parker's forever, and besides, I loved my house. It just so happened that something unpleasant had happened here, but I felt I had to face it in order to move on.

He climbed out of the truck and came around to open the door. Grabbing my hand, he helped me down.

"I'm going to check the place out and make sure everything is safe before I leave." We walked hand in hand up the walkway.

"What are you going to do while I'm at work?" he questioned.

"I was going to hit the gym, do some laundry, and maybe watch a movie."

He took the keys from my hand and unlocked the front door, then held it open for me, smacking me lightly on the ass as I walked through in front of him. Grabbing me around the waist he kissed me on the back of the neck.

I followed him as he checked out the house. The last room we came to was my bedroom. He was making sure the slider was locked as I stood staring at the bed. The blankets were still messed from that night. I could feel my heart start to race, and I was getting cold, the room starting to spin.

"You should be good now." He turned to look at me, concern growing on his face.

I stood staring at the bed, where Dean had attacked me.

"Tatum, did you hear me?"

"Hmmm?"

He frowned at me.

"Yes, I heard you. I should be good." I shook out of my stare and looked to Parker.

"Are you sure you want to stay here? You don't have to," he said, coming around from the far side of the bed and wrapping me in his strong arms.

"No, I do. I can't let myself be afraid of him anymore," I said while buried in his chest, his warmth soothing me.

"Well, you know I'm a call or text away. Elliott and I will be in the next district over. I'll have one of the guys drive by tonight?"

"No, Parker, it's not necessary." I knew I was preaching to the choir. He would do whatever it took to make me feel safe.

"I'll come by after I get off shift. We can go for breakfast in the morning." He gave me a final squeeze and headed to the front door.

Taking my spare key from the drawer I placed it in his hand. "Just come in when you get off shift." I reached up and gave him a soft kiss. "See you in the morning." He walked to his truck, waving as he backed out of the driveway.

As soon as Parker was gone, I walked back into my bedroom. A chill ran through my body just being in there alone. I kept feeling as if Dean was standing behind me. I wouldn't be able to sleep on these sheets or with these blankets until they were clean.

Quickly, I stripped everything and separated the loads. After everything was in the wash, I filled a bucket with hot water and went in to mop the floors. Funny as it was, I could still smell Dean in the room even after everything had been cleaned.

I continued throughout the house, washing all the

floors. Finally, the silence was getting to me, so I turned the radio on and filled the house with happy music. Once the loads of wash were switched, I headed to the kitchen to make myself something to eat. It was already four, and I was starving. Parker had started at two and was only two hours into his twelve-hour shift. Opening the fridge, I realized after I ate, a trip to the market would be in order.

It was such a beautiful afternoon that I decided to walk to the market. The wind off the bay was cool and soothing after all the hard work I had done. Bags in hand, I turned the outside light on and locked the door. Taking a look around, I started off in the direction of the market. I noticed a black car parked on the opposite side of the road. It looked as if someone was sitting in the driver's seat. I took a deep breath. I needed to stop being paranoid. He was in jail.

Ten minutes later, I walked into the market's parking lot. I headed inside and grabbed some groceries—not too much, just enough to be able to carry home and feed me until I could do a proper shop. I paid for my sale and headed home. Walking out of the market, I saw the same black car sitting across the parking lot. This time, there was definitely someone sitting in the front seat.

I kept my eye on the car and could feel my heart start to race. Taking a deep breath, I focused on getting home. Why hadn't I driven? After walking a little way up the road, I checked back over my shoulder. The car was pulling out of the parking lot and headed in my direction.

"It's all in your head. The guy probably had to go to the store," I told myself. I reached into my pocket to text

Parker and realized at that moment I had left my cell phone on my charger. "Shit." I picked up my pace.

Breathless with anxiety, I walked up my driveway and looked back over my shoulder. There parked on the side of the road across the street was the very car with the same silhouette of a man sitting in the driver's seat.

I started to shake and had a hard time getting the key into the lock. Once inside, I shut and locked the front door, dropped the groceries, and slid down the door. Pulling my knees into my chest, I wrapped my arms around them and started to cry.

As soon as I finally pulled myself together, I grabbed my phone and dialed Parker's number. It went to voicemail, so I tried Elliott—same thing. They were both busy. I typed out a text to both of them and got up off the floor. When I checked across the street, the car was gone.

"You're being crazy. He is in jail," I said aloud to myself.

I pulled the blind closed on the window over the sink anyway and put away the few things I had bought. I kept getting the feeling that someone was standing behind me and kept glancing over my shoulder. I was going to drive myself crazy. I had worked myself up so much. I put the kettle on and ordered a pizza for dinner before making my bed and closing all the curtains in the bedroom and living room.

I went to pour the hot water into my mug and jumped at the sound of a knock on the door, causing me to spill hot water all over the counter.

I set the kettle down and checked through the peep-hole. It was only the pizza guy. Opening the door, I slipped him the money and took the pizza. Before shutting the door, I glanced up and down the road again. I wanted to see if that black car was still there, but it was gone. Locking up the door, I flipped the outside light on for Parker and took my tea and pizza into the living room. I quickly changed into my shorts and tank top and curled up under a blanket on the couch to watch a movie.

I checked my cell phone during the first commercial and saw a message from Parker.

PARKER: BEN DROVE BY YOUR PLACE, BEEN PATROLLING THE AREA ON AND OFF, NO SIGN OF BLACK CAR. WILL KEEP CHECKING. IF YOU NEED TO, GO TO MY PLACE. SEE YOU IN A BIT, PRETTY BUSY TONIGHT.

PARKER

I PUT MY PHONE DOWN AND CHECKED THE TIME. IT WAS almost ten. I turned to Elliott who took a sip of his coffee and punched a message into his phone. He was grinning like an idiot when another response pinged in.

"Jen again?"

"Yeah. How's Tatum doing?" he asked, putting the phone down.

"I don't know. I'm worried about her. I don't know if I should have left her there alone. Ben says there's no black car, and there hasn't been one all night. But she's insisting that she was followed to the market and home again tonight. I've had him patrolling the area all night."

The thought of her freaking out by herself was almost too much for me to handle. I was still pissed I had missed her call, but we were in the middle of an arrest. I couldn't stop what was going on and answer.

"I know; she sent me a text as well. She's so damn stubborn. You'd never have been able to talk her out of staying there. You know that. But I do agree with you, it may be too soon for her to stay alone, but I swear you'd never convince her, so don't beat yourself up over it."

He took a bite of his burger. It was the first chance we'd had to stop and have dinner all night.

He was right, I had to stop. As much as I wanted to protect her, I couldn't do it if she wasn't willing to be protected.

"I was thinking of taking her away this weekend, go down to my parents' cottage. Would that be okay with you?"

"Parker, man, you know I've always approved of you being with Tatum. You don't need my permission if you want to date my sister. I think taking her away is a good idea. She needs it, get herself back together." He chuckled and checked his phone, typing in another message.

"Are things pretty serious between the two of you?" I asked before taking a bite of my burger.

"Yeah. I think I may ask her to move in with me. This long-distance thing is going to be too hard. I want to be with her."

My phone buzzed in my pocket. Looking down at the screen, I saw a new message from Tatum.

TATUM: HEADING TO BED, I'VE LEFT THE
LIGHT ON FOR YOU

PARKER: BE HOME BEFORE YOU KNOW IT

Putting my phone down, I took a drink of my coffee and leaned my head back against the headrest. "Let's hope we don't get any more calls tonight. I'm beat."

My phone buzzed again. Checking the screen, a new message appeared.

BEN: BLACK AUDI IS PARKED OUTSIDE ACROSS
THE STREET, PULLED OVER WATCHING TO SEE
IF ANYONE GETS OUT.

PARKER: LET ME KNOW.

"Fuck, Ben just sent me a text. There is a black Audi sitting across the street. Ben's keeping a lookout."

I wanted to get over there, but if we got caught leaving our district, we'd be fucked.

"Do you have any time you can take? We could always take off early," I said, looking over and seeing Elliott's face buried in his phone.

"Yeah, lots of time. How about we head back to the station?"

I PULLED MY TRUCK INTO TATUM'S DRIVEWAY. THE front light was on. Ben had sent a text to me twenty minutes ago and let me know the car had finally left. I locked up the truck and walked to the front door, putting the key in the lock.

Once inside, I shut the outside light off and locked the door then made my way down the hall, trying to be quiet so I didn't wake her. I stopped just outside the bedroom door, shut my phone off, and emptied my pockets, leaving everything on top of the entertainment unit.

I went to take another step, the floor creaking underneath my weight, and heard Tatum scream, "Get the fuck out! Cops are on their way."

I pushed the door open and saw Tatum curled under the blankets. Quickly, I kneeled on the bed and grabbed hold of her arms. She kicked at me and let out a blood-curdling scream.

"Tatum, it's me. It's just me. Calm down." I ripped the blankets off her and grabbed her, pulling her into me. "It's just me."

She was breathing hard and was incredibly sweaty. Pulling her tight against my chest, I tried to calm her down.

"Parker?" She finally stilled.

"It's just me, baby. You okay?" She began to cry while I held her in my arms.

"I...I...I have been watching the black car all night. It wouldn't leave." Her chest heaved.

"It's okay. Ben was watching. I thought you went to bed at ten?"

"I did. I got into bed and started hearing things. I tried hard to shut it out of my mind, but it got worse and worse."

"I'm sorry I scared you, but I figured you were asleep. We took a couple hours off early. I didn't want you to be alone any longer." I nestled her head into the crook of my shoulder and held her, smoothing her hair.

It didn't take long to calm her down, but she was so warm. I wanted her to cool off before going to bed, so I picked her up and carried her to the shower.

TATUM

I PULLED MY WET HAIR UP INTO A PONYTAIL, THREW ON a T-shirt, and went into the kitchen to make us both a cup of tea.

"I missed you tonight," I heard from behind me.

"I missed you too." I felt his hands run over my upper arms and start massaging my shoulders.

"I want you to know you're safe with me," he whispered into my ear.

I closed my eyes and relaxed into him, letting the tension from the day seep out of my aching muscles. "I know that."

Turning me around, he grabbed me under the ass,

picked me up and set me on the counter. He angled his towel-wrapped body between my legs. His hand gently brushed my cheek, leaned in, and placed his lips against mine, his tongue finding its way into my mouth. I wrapped my arms around his neck, and he pulled me closer into his body and deepened the kiss. I let out a soft moan. I loved kissing this man.

Kissing and sucking on my ear and neck, I closed my eyes and breathed in the smell of him. The feel of his lips on my neck drove me crazy. Picking me up off the counter, he carried me into the other room and out onto the back deck. He placed me down on the deck, still holding onto my hand. He sat down on one of the lounge chairs and coaxed me to straddle his lap.

"I want to take you away this weekend, to my parents' cottage, get you away from here for a bit. What do you say?"

"Elliott and I are supposed to be hanging out this weekend."

"I've already cleared it with him; he said to go. So you're all mine."

I smiled, leaning my forehead against his. I could feel his arousal through the towel hitting me in just the right spot. I ground down on him and kissed him again. His hands massaged my breasts, his thumbs rubbing over my tightened nipples.

"Lift your arms over your head," his said, his voice quiet.

I was hesitant and looked over my shoulder in case anyone was out on the beach.

"There is no one out there, baby," he whispered.

Doing as he asked, I removed my T-shirt, casting it off to the side. He sat forward, taking my nipple into his mouth and sucking hard. I let out a whimper as he swirled his tongue around my nipple and then switched to the other side, gently biting and sucking.

"I love these," he whispered. Placing his hand between my legs, his thumb found my clit. He rubbed me through my soaked panties with enough pressure to make me moan. "Baby, you're so wet. Fuck, I love it," he whispered against my neck as he continued to rub me. "I want you on top of me now," he said into my mouth. Shoving my panties to the side, he undid the towel from around his waist.

I rose onto my knees, and he positioned himself at my opening. Gripping my hips, he guided me down on him, every inch stretching me. A quiver went through me once I was seated on him.

"Fuck, you're so tight," he said, caressing my back and sitting still until I was used to him being there.

When I was ready, I ground down on him as he thrust up and into me. He pulled me down to meet my mouth.

"I want to feel you come, baby," he whispered into my ear, sucking the lobe into his mouth.

My release came quickly in this position. I tightened around him, and a deep groan came from his lips, his thrusts getting faster and deeper before he filled me. Collapsing against him, he held me while staying inside of me, kissing my shoulder, until we both caught our breath.

"Ready for bed, sweetie?"

I nodded.

I curled into Parker's arms and rested my head on his chest. He held me tight against him and kissed the top of my head. Rolling me onto my back, he rose up on his forearm and leaned down and kissed me slow and deep.

"You know what I'd like?" he asked, looking into my eyes.

I shook my head.

"You. Again." He reached up and turned off the light on my nightstand, and his lips met my mouth.

Chapter Twenty

Tatum

PARKER FINISHED SECURING THE BOAT TO THE DOCK, AND
then handed me our bags and the cooler before climbing
off the boat.

"You're sure your parents are okay with us using their
place this weekend?" I asked.

"Yep, they aren't able to be here this weekend, so they
said it was all ours." He picked up the cooler while I
grabbed our bags.

There were only four cottages on this island which
would make for a quiet getaway. We walked up the dock,
and in the distance, I could see a little wooden cottage
nestled amongst the trees. The sun had already set, and it
was getting dark and a little cool.

"Come on, we better get on inside. It's supposed to be a

cooler night tonight. I want to make sure I get a good fire going," Parker said, nodding toward the cottage.

I followed along, taking in my surroundings. I noticed a cottage off to the far left of us, lights shining in the windows, and I could smell a fire burning.

Parker unlocked the door and turned the lights on. We were in a huge great room with a great big, stone fireplace. A TV hung over the mantel. A full-size kitchen was off to the right, and a staircase in the back led up to the bedrooms.

"This place is beautiful," I said, taking in the surroundings.

I followed Parker as he took the cooler over to the kitchen and set it on the floor by the fridge.

"I'm just going to grab wood from outside. Did you want to unpack the cooler?"

I nodded, taking in the look in his eyes, desire radiating between us. He gave me a soft kiss before heading outside. I busied myself emptying the cooler and the few bags of food we had brought from the store. Parker brought in four armfuls of wood, and then locked the door.

"What room are we staying in? I will take our bags up."

"First one at the top of the stairs."

"Okay." Picking up the bags, I carried them up to the top of the stairs, opened the bedroom door and turned the lights on. The room was spacious yet cozy and warm, decorated in dark greens with a great big king-size bed. I set the bags down at the end of the bed and walked over to look out the window. It was beautiful here.

Unzipping my bag, I pulled out a pair of yoga pants and

a T-shirt and got changed. Exhausted from being up for the past few days, I was craving relaxation. Once I changed, I headed back downstairs. The lights had been dimmed, and soft music floated through the air. Parker was in the living room sitting on the floor with two glasses of white wine sitting on the table. He had pulled out a blanket and laid it out on the thick rug in front of the fireplace. Piles of pillows and cushions from the couch were spread out on the floor.

He patted the spot beside him. "Come make yourself comfortable."

He looked so handsome with the firelight bouncing off his tanned skin.

I sat down beside him, leaning back into the cloud of pillows. He reached over and handed me a glass of wine.

"Thank you." I took the glass from him and took a sip. Setting the glass down, I relaxed back into the pillows, closed my eyes, and soaked in the warmth of the fire. I was exhausted.

After a few minutes, I could feel his gaze upon me. I opened my eyes and felt a flush of warmth spread through me from the way he was looking at me.

"What is it?" I asked.

"You're just so beautiful," he replied.

I grew quiet. In the year we had dated, Dean had never uttered those words to me, and it made me uneasy to hear them. I sat staring into the fire, holding my wine glass in my hands and taking the occasional sip.

Parker's hand went to my shoulder. "Tatum?"

"Please don't say that." I sniffled, unable to look at him.

Even though the bruises from the first attack had healed, the invisible ones were still there; along with all the horrible words that Dean had shoved at me every chance he got.

Parker brought his hand to my face and brushed the strands of hair away that had fallen into my eyes. "Tell me why?"

"Look at me." Tears spilled from my eyes and streamed down my face. I didn't feel beautiful, but I guess that's what happened. I had started to believe everything he said —how useless I was and how no one would want me. He never once complimented me on anything.

"Yes, look at you. My beautiful girl." He brought his hand to my cheek and turned my face up. "Don't cry." Looking into my eyes, his thumbs wiped the tears away, and he brought his lips to mine. He lay beside me, pulled me into his arms, and held me.

PARKER

WHEN I WOKE UP, THE FIRE HAD DIED DOWN TO A PILE of glowing embers. We had fallen asleep on the floor. Unwrapping Tatum from my body, I got up and quietly put more wood on the fire then turned and watched her sleep. She was finally resting peacefully.

I went into the washroom to wash my hands after handling the wood before returning to her. Shutting the door, I flipped the light on and looked at myself in the mirror.

Tell her the truth. Man up and tell her you love her. I took a deep breath. I had been fighting with myself since the first night I stayed at her place. I guess no matter how much time passed, when your heart knows it knows.

When I returned, Tatum was still on her stomach under the blankets, her eyes closed. I crawled in beside her and adjusted the pillows behind me. I placed my hands under my head and closed my eyes. Tatum placed her hand across my abs and curled up against me. "Did I wake you?" I asked, wrapping my arm around her.

She placed a light kiss on my shoulder and ran her hand down my abs. She reached down and gripped my cock through my boxers. Fire lit through me at her gentle touch. I sat up and rolled her onto her back, kissing her hard. Lifting her back up off the floor, I pulled her T-shirt off and laid her back onto the pillows. Kissing down her neck and over her breasts, I ran my hands down her body and removed her pants, going back up to run my tongue over her nipples again.

Her head tilted back into the pillows. She was biting on her bottom lip, trying hard to stifle the moan that I heard slip between her lips. Kissing down her stomach, I placed myself between her legs and pushed them open, letting them fall to the side, and sat back to look at her spread before me.

The firelight glistened off her sex. I could feel saliva pool in my mouth. I couldn't wait to taste her again. Holding her legs open, I leaned down and ran my tongue through her folds and heard a guttural moan from her lips. My hunger for her growing, I sucked her clit into my mouth. I inserted a finger into her tight pussy and hooked my finger, rubbing her in the right place.

"Come for me." I sucked her clit back into my mouth and alternated between sucking and running my tongue over it. I felt her clench around my finger, and her juices flooded my mouth. Breathing hard, she relaxed back into the pillows.

I watched her as I crawled up between her legs and placed my cock at her entrance, running it through her juices. She looked up at me with those beautiful hazel eyes as I kissed her. Lining myself up with her entrance, I slid into her. She moaned into my mouth and wrapped her legs around my back as I pumped into her. I could feel her tighten around my cock almost instantly, nearly sending me over the edge, but I held back.

She laid her legs over my thighs, and I sat back on my knees, keeping myself deeply planted in her. With my thumb, I started rubbing her swollen clit. Deeply pumping into her, I could feel myself about to let go as she tightened again around my cock. I gave two final, hard pumps and filled her. Collapsing on her, I kissed her softly. Once I caught my breath, I pulled out. I got up and went to the washroom and cleaned myself up then brought a wet cloth to her and cleaned her off.

Lying beside her, I pulled her into my arms. We lay in total silence for a while, listening to the sounds of our breathing and our heartbeats.

"Tatum?"

"Yes," she whispered.

"I wanted to tell you that..." I swallowed hard, that knot in my stomach returning, and suddenly I went quiet.

"Parker?" I loved the sound of my name come from her lips. "What is it?"

"I love you." The knot disappeared almost instantly. I had finally said it, and I prayed that she said it back to me, but she was almost too quiet. I waited a few seconds, the delay almost killing me. Looking over at her, I could see her eyes glistening. "I love you," I repeated.

I heard her sniffle. "I love you too."

Chapter Twenty-One

Tatum

PARKER PULLED INTO THE DRIVEWAY AND SHUT HIS truck off. It had been a great weekend away with him, but today he had to work. He hopped out of the truck and pulled my duffel bag from the back and walked me to the door. Bringing my bag in, he did a quick check of the house to make sure no one was there. I wasn't sure if he was doing it to calm my fears or his.

"Okay, baby, all is good. If you need me tonight, just send me a message okay?" He leaned against the doorframe and bent down to meet my lips.

Pressing into my mouth ever so gently, he wrapped his arm around my waist and pulled me into him. He trailed kisses to my ear and down my neck, and I could feel his arousal against me. "Parker, you've got to go, sweetie. You're going to be late."

"But you're worth being late for," he said between kissing and sucking on my bottom lip. He glanced down at his watch, noticing the time. "Okay, you're right. I've got to go. I love you."

"I love you too."

He smiled and placed another kiss on my lips. "I'll see you later tonight, baby. I'll call you when I'm done with my shift."

I watched as he walked to his truck, climbed in, and waved as he drove down the street. I was completely in love with everything about him, and that was scaring me. I smiled to myself as I closed the front door and turned to put the kettle on. I needed some time to relax and sort out my feelings.

I popped a tea bag in my mug and grabbed a piece of fruit from the fridge then carried my duffel bag into the bedroom and made my way back to the kitchen to make my tea. I decided to unpack later and curled up on the couch in front of the TV.

THE RINGING PHONE STARTLED ME OUT OF A DEAD SLEEP. It was starting to get dark outside, and I wondered how long I had been asleep. Looking at the clock, it was already four-thirty. I had been asleep for the better part of the day. I took a drink of my cold tea and grabbed the receiver. "Hello?"

"Tatum, it's Brad Keller calling. How have you been?"

I was surprised to hear from him.

I perked up. "Mr. Keller, I'm doing well. How about yourself?"

"I'm well. Listen, Tatum, the reason for my call is I have an opportunity for you, and I'm hoping that you have a few minutes to discuss."

I smiled into the phone. Nothing would make me happier than to get back to work. After all, it would get my mind off all that had happened with Dean.

"Of course, I'd be happy to hear about it."

"I was hoping you would say that. The restructure is complete, and we are currently working on assembling a new team. I thought of you right away for the position. I'm in need of a department editor."

I was shocked. I had been working toward that position for the last seven years. "Well, I'm definitely interested. Would I be able to do the position from home here?"

"Unfortunately, no. I'm afraid you would need to be at the office daily. I know that you have moved, but I would like to see you give this position a great deal of consideration. The position wouldn't start for another month. We are running some major meetings for the next couple of weeks.

"If you decided you would like to take the position, we would need you to be present for those. We will arrange for you to have a room at one of the hotels, that way, you'd have time to find a place and be able to arrange to move back. If it took you extra time to find a new place, then I'd be willing to extend you a couple extra weeks to get settled."

The line went quiet. I wasn't sure what to say. Things with Parker were just starting again. It seemed as if, once again, something was stepping in and putting an end to us. "When would you need me there for these meetings?" I asked, swallowing hard.

"Monday morning at eight o'clock. I'm sorry about the short notice, but it took me a while to get a hold of your new number."

Monday morning. That was in three days. I would have to leave, at the latest, Sunday evening. How would I explain this to Parker? My stomach started rolling. I wasn't sure I wanted us to end.

"What do you say, Tatum? Will you join the team?"

I could feel my eyes starting to sting. I had been working toward this position. I couldn't possibly turn it down, could I? "I'll see you Monday morning, Mr. Keller." The words fell out of my mouth before I had a chance to stop them. A single tear traveled down my cheek.

"I will call you with your flight and hotel details. I'll see you Monday, Tatum. Congratulations."

"Mr. Keller, you can just leave the details of the flight on my home number. I will send you an email with the number."

"Thanks, Tatum. Have a great evening."

I hung up the phone and put my head in my hands. I had no idea what I had just done. If worse came to worst, I could always reject the opportunity if I found it wasn't for me. My phone chimed with a message. I grabbed it and saw an incoming text from Parker. My hands started to shake as I opened his message.

PARKER: I'M ON MY WAY HOME, THINK YOU CAN BE READY IN TWENTY, I THOUGHT A NICE DINNER IS IN ORDER, I MISSED MY BABY TODAY.

I typed out a quick reply and went to jump in the shower and get ready for dinner. There was no point telling him tonight. I didn't want to ruin our evening. It would be bad enough when I finally had to tell him.

I UNLOCKED THE FRONT DOOR AND HEADED INTO THE kitchen, Parker following close behind. I could feel his eyes on me as I went to the coffee maker, pouring some grounds into a filter. I felt his hands rub up my arms.

"Did you want a coffee?"

I felt his hands run back down my arms and his hot breath on my neck. His kiss on the back of my neck was like a bolt of electricity that shot through right to my center. Closing my eyes, I leaned back into him and reached my hands behind my head and into his hair. He ran his hands up my stomach and over my breasts, my nipples hardening under his touch. He spun me around and lifted me up onto the kitchen counter, and I wrapped my legs around his waist.

"Guess not," I mumbled as his lips found mine, his tongue exploring my mouth.

Finally, he lifted me off the counter and carried me into the bedroom and laid me on the bed. He stood over me and pulled his shirt off. I could never get enough of his chest—so well defined, his shoulders so broad, and those abs.

Reaching down, he undid the button on my jeans and lifted my top to kiss my stomach. He lifted me off the bed and pulled my pants off my body. I pulled my top over my head and met his lips as they came crashing down on me.

I reached my hand down and undid the first button on his jeans. I could feel how hard he was through the stiff material, and my hand ran over it and squeezed his hard cock.

"Take these off," I moaned, wanting to feel him.

He slid himself out of his jeans and boxers. Reaching down, I could feel the wetness at the tip of his cock as I ran my hand over the soft skin. A deep, raspy moan came from him as I ran my hand over him again.

"Jesus, I love it when you do that, but you've got to stop. I want to last longer than five minutes. I wanted you all through dinner," he said, chuckling.

Kneeling on the floor between my legs, he ran his hands over my hips. He grabbed the waistband of my panties and pulled them off my body, trailing kissing down my thighs. He stopped and took a deep breath, his eyes wandering from my face down my body. He placed his hands on my knees and pushed my legs open. His hands ran up my legs from my knees to my thighs. He looked me directly in my eyes as he leaned forward and placed a kiss right on my inner thigh. My breath hitched as he kissed the other inner thigh, and then he blew on my soaked, throbbing center.

"Get on your knees, baby. I want to feel what it's like to take you from behind."

I rolled onto my hands and knees, and his hands grasped my hips as he pulled me back into him. He placed himself at my entrance and slid deep inside of me, filling me deeper than before. He pumped into me, slow and soft at first, and then a little harder.

"My God, you feel amazing on my cock." He brought his hand around and started stroking my clit as he fucked me.

I could feel his cock throbbing inside of me as I tightened around him, my release coming hard. He pulled himself out of me and lay down on his side, and I curled myself into him. Smoothing my hair, he wrapped his arm around my waist and placed a kiss on my ear.

"I love you," he whispered into my ear.

As the words fell from his lips, I felt as if someone punched me in the gut. I should have told him about that phone call.

"I love you too."

After Parker had fallen off to sleep, I lay staring at the ceiling. This wasn't how this was supposed to go. I wasn't supposed to fall in love with him, and I certainly didn't know how to tell him that I had accepted this position.

The nagging feeling in my gut wasn't settling and was starting to make me feel sick. I didn't want to lose him again, but I feared that once I told him, he'd be gone. I rolled onto my side and watched him sleep. I was afraid this would be the last time I would see him like this, and I wanted to etch this memory of him in my mind.

The phone woke me out of a dead sleep. Parker was still asleep and had me securely wrapped in his arms. I went to reach for the phone, but he grabbed my arm.

"Let the machine get it. I want you," he moaned, pulling me back down and kissing me deep.

He quickly distracted me from the ringing phone. The machine kicked on, and as soon as he heard the voice, he stilled, listening.

"Tatum, it's Brad Keller calling. Your flight has been arranged for tomorrow at four pm. You're staying in room four-twelve at the Marriott. See you Monday morning at eight sharp. I'm glad you took me up on the offer. I look forward to working with you once again."

The dial tone blared through the machine.

I wasn't sure what it was that I saw in Parker's eyes, but I knew if I hadn't already been lying down, his look would have knocked me to the floor.

"What was that about, Tatum?"

I was on the verge of crying and throwing up.

"Tatum?" He sat up and put his head into his hands. "Are you leaving?"

Another moment of panic shot through me. Tears burning my eyes, I nodded. I couldn't get anything else out; tears ran down my cheeks as I blinked.

"So, what has this been between you and me? A game? Are you trying to get back at me?"

I shook my head, trying to find the words to explain myself.

"Did you think that I wouldn't be upset or that I didn't deserve to know? When did they call, Tatum?" he demanded. Getting up out of the bed, he bent over and grabbed his jeans from the floor.

"They called yesterday. I was going to tell you. I was. I just wasn't sure how." I sniffled.

"So instead you pretended like nothing was going on and let me find out this way? It's nice to know what I mean to you. Let me ask you, was that just a reflex *I love you*? Felt like you needed to say it, so I didn't get hurt?"

I put my head in my hands and started to cry.

"When were you planning to tell me? When you boarded the plane or while I was at work?"

I could barely see him through my teary eyes. He wasn't angry; he was hurt. I had done it again.

"Parker please, let me explain. It's not what you're thinking, really. Please just wait."

He put his pants on and grabbed his shirt from my dresser. "I've got to go, Tatum. Have a safe trip."

He walked out of the bedroom, and within seconds, I heard the front door slam shut. I rolled onto my side and buried my face in my pillow and sobbed.

I SPENT MOST OF THE DAY AND EVENING IN BED, FINALLY getting up to pack. Elliott had been calling, no doubt to find out what the hell went on, but I ignored the phone. I pulled the suitcase from the closet and threw in some clothes. I only needed work clothes. After all, I was only going to be gone for two weeks.

Once I had most of the clothes packed, I grabbed my toiletry bag and threw that into my suitcase. Sitting down on the edge of my bed, I glanced around the room, doubt creeping into my mind. I wasn't sure this was the right move to be making. Less than twelve hours ago, I had everything I'd wanted right here in this room, and now he was gone.

Reaching for my cell phone, I typed out a message to Parker and sat waiting for a reply. And waiting. I could feel the tears start building again. This move was a mistake, I could feel it to my core.

I called Elliott back. "Well, it's about time you called me back." The tone of his voice told me he knew what had happened.

"Have you heard from Parker?" I asked quietly.

"Yes, he told me you were flying out tomorrow. Where are you going?"

"Work called me back. They had an amazing offer for me...or what I thought was an amazing offer."

"So, you thought you would take it?"

"Well, I thought I would try it out. I haven't made a final decision yet." I choked.

"Well, it sounded final when Parker talked to me. He said you didn't have much to say on the subject except that you had accepted the offer."

I dropped my head and pinched the bridge of my nose. I could feel a headache coming on.

"He told me that you didn't even tell him. He found out from a message left on your machine. What's going on with you?"

I hated hearing the disappointment in his voice. "I don't know. I have worked so hard for this. I was one of the only ones they called back. I didn't know how to tell him. I didn't want to hurt him, or you, for that matter."

"Well, congrats to you. You don't need to worry about hurting me, but you should have at least considered Parker's feelings. You realize that he has never gotten over you. You can't do this to him. Also, Tatum, after all that's gone on, how are we going to protect you there once Dean gets released? Did you think about that?"

"Elliott, don't make me feel worse than I already do. I don't need protecting. Dean is behind bars."

"Well, someone needs to knock some kind of sense into you. I'm pissed with you! Your stubborn attitude is what got you into the mess you're in with this asshole. If you had come to me when it all started between you and Dean, you wouldn't be in the position to need protecting."

"You're not being fair to me. I'll be fine."

"Yeah, sure, as of right now, you are fine. You're right, but once he's released, you won't be. I see this shit happen all the time. You do realize that once he is released, he will be sent back to the city until his court date. I don't want something to happen to you."

"Nothing is going to happen to me. I'm going to go to there for two weeks, work, and see what happens. That's it. Besides, the officer told me that if he is released, he'll have to stay away from me."

Elliott let out a deep breath. "Fuck, Tatum, I see these things happen all the time. Girl thinks she is safe, guy gets released, and the first thing he does is track her down and shows her who is boss, regardless of what conditions he has on him when he is released. These fucks don't give a shit, because if they did, these things wouldn't happen. The last one I saw didn't end so well, and I don't want to see you end up like her."

I could hear the added frustration in his voice.

"Elliott, it's enough. Now, could you tell me how to get a hold of Parker please?" I was getting angrier by the second. Even though he had every right to talk to me that way, I didn't want to hear it.

"He told me he was going away for a bit. He doesn't want to be bothered by anyone."

I huffed into the phone. "All right, well, my flight leaves tomorrow at four." The line went quiet. I wasn't sure Elliott was even on the other end of the phone. "Elliott?"

"Have a good trip. I guess I'll see you in a couple of weeks." I heard the dreaded click on the other end of the phone, the familiar feeling of regret sinking in.

THEY WERE CALLING OUT THE SEATS TO BOARD THE plane. Elliott hadn't answered his cell when I tried to call him earlier. I wanted to know everything was okay between us. I had called Parker as well, but he still hadn't returned my messages. I hoped to hear his voice before I left. I wanted to have a chance to explain the situation.

I dialed his number again, but the phone rang and rang, his deep voice finally coming over the line. I left one more message before boarding the plane. "Parker, it's me. I'm sorry you had to find out the way you did. I'm sure you don't even want to hear from me, but I wanted to say I love you. I'm in love with you. Please call me."

As I pressed the end call, I heard the last boarding call for my flight. I handed the boarding agent my pass and headed down the ramp to the plane.

Chapter Twenty-Two

Dean

I walked out of building and got into the black
Audi sitting out front. "What have you found out since
I've been in that hell hole?"

"Sir, you're not going to like it. It appears she is
involved with another man."

"Who? Tell me it's not that fucking cop." He didn't
answer me. "So, it is that asshole cop?"

"Yes, sir. I watched her have sex with him on the back
deck of her place."

My hands balled into tight fists as I listened to what he
said. She was mine and would remain mine. I had to teach
her a lesson.

"Where is she now? Take me there."

"Sir, you just got out of jail, sir. How about we wait."

My jaw clenched. "I said take me to her. That bitch needs a lesson."

"Sir—"

"Do you know where she is or has your dumb ass lost her?"

"She's in the city, alone. I have McKay watching her. She's at the Marriott."

"Take me there now!" I barked.

He started the car and pulled away from the curb. I couldn't wait to get my hands on that little bitch.

Chapter Twenty-Three

Tatum

I was more tired than normal when I returned to the hotel room. It had been a long day full of meetings. I walked in and kicked my shoes off. I was still undecided about what I would do—move back or return to my new home. It was a privilege that they thought to call me back, but I was beginning to seriously doubt if working at this pace was for me.

I sat on the bed and rubbed my aching feet. I still had three hours of work to complete that was due in the morning before I could curl up in bed. Changing out of my clothes, I changed into my T-shirt and pajama pants and grabbed the room service menu. Eating out all the time was going to add on the pounds.

Calling down, I ordered a quinoa salad with a side of

salmon and pulled my laptop from the bag. I was about to start writing when my phone rang.

"Hey, Jen." I smiled.

"Hey, babe, how's things going?"

"I'm so tired. I don't remember ever being this tired. And if you really want to know, I am so bloated, my feet are killing me. My period is five days late. I am never late! Oh, and to top it off, I spent the first three hours of my day running to the bathroom. It's all stressing me out big time!"

"Oh, girl, have you never learned. Stressing over it only makes it stay away longer. Do you remember that time in college when I slept with Rob, Eric, and then that mystery man at that party all in the same month? My period was so late, I made myself sick every morning for three weeks convincing myself I was doomed. I was going to have to drop out of college and become a single mom.

"You were so awesome, you went and bought almost every pregnancy test on campus. As soon as I was done taking them all to get the same answer of negative, my period started the next hour."

We both laughed at the memory.

I had always loved her and was thankful to have her here to talk to. "So, your advice is to buy every pregnancy test in the hotel pharmacy?"

"No, my advice is take a load off. It's from all the stress you've been under. Drink some wine, put your feet up, and relax! Maybe a spa day is in order. Anyway, I'll come over tomorrow night with dinner. We can drink some wine, watch a movie. Possibly, I'll bring a test and be a good friend to you like you were to me." She laughed into the phone. "Have you made a decision about the job yet?"

"I'm still not sure what I'm going to do. I've wanted this position for years." I sighed into the phone. "What about you? Have you made a decision about you and Elliott?"

Elliott had asked Jen to move in with him. I didn't know how I felt about that. If she moved in with him, and I stayed here, then I would be alone.

"I told him yes. He is planning to come up with Parker to help me move most of my stuff."

I didn't want to talk about Parker. I was missing him more than I cared to admit to myself.

"When?"

"The end of the month. I can't wait to be with him."

"Don't you think it's a little soon to move in together? I mean you've only spent one weekend together." I could sense the jealousy in my voice and hoped she didn't pick up on it.

"If it doesn't work out then I will chalk it up to another one of the dumbest things I ever did. But sometimes you have to take a chance. I'm still young; I can afford to make mistakes." She laughed.

That was one thing I admired about Jen — her spontaneity. She had never been afraid to put herself out there and try something, even when the odds were against her.

"I wish it worked out for me that way."

"I thought things were going well between you both? What happened?"

I hadn't mentioned anything to Jen about what had

happened. "Things were going so well, until Saturday. When the call came in to come back to work, I didn't know how to tell him. I mean, they called on Friday and wanted me to start on Monday. I decided I just wanted to forget about it and enjoy our date that night, so I didn't tell him." I swallowed.

"We went out, he came back and spent the night. The next morning, Keller called and left a message about my flight. Parker heard it and got pissed. He asked me what the call was about, and I froze. I couldn't answer his questions.

"He left. He thought I had been playing a game with him to get back at him for what happened when we were younger. I called Elliott to see if he knew where Parker was —I didn't want to leave without talking to him—and Elliott pretty much gave me shit. I've left Parker messages, but he hasn't called me back."

"Give him some time. Call again in a couple of days. Considering how he feels about you, I am sure he will call you back when he is ready."

"What do you mean by that?"

"It's not a secret he still loves you, Tatum. Don't be so blind. I could see it written all over him the first time I saw him. The way he looked at you was the same way he looked at you back in college."

I grew quiet. I was scared. Scared of losing him, scared of loving him, scared for what it all meant. A knock interrupted my thoughts. I opened the door and room service came walking in with my food. As soon as the door was closed, the smell of salmon permeated the room and my stomach did a flip.

"I think I am going to lose my mind over all this restaurant food, Jen, honestly."

"Why don't you come and stay with me then. It'll be like old times. You can help me pack, and I'll help you relax." She laughed into the phone.

"I don't want to intrude, Jen. I have a ton of work to do every night. I need to make up my mind about what I am going to do as well. If I'm going to stay, I will have to sell that place. I can't afford to keep it and an apartment in the city."

"My God, would you stop? You're not an intrusion. You're my best friend! You know what? I think you need to be more like me and go for what you want. Is this what you want?"

I stood staring at my laptop, paperwork spread all over the desk. I was missing Parker. I was missing the comfort I had felt in the last few weeks being around him. I looked at the food getting cold on the table, the smell making me nauseous. Was this worth it? I had exactly six days left to make that decision.

"I don't know, Jen. I am trying. The offer is great."

"Who are you kidding, you sound miserable! I say you get your ass back down to the most awesome man you have ever known before you throw it all away again. Over something I know you don't really want." She knew me too well.

"I'll know by the end of the week."

"Bullshit, you already know, you coward. You just need the guts to admit to yourself that you need him."

I smiled into the phone. This was exactly why I loved her—she called me on all my shit.

I took a breath. She was right. I wanted to be back in his arms. "I have until Friday. I'll make my decision by that time. For now, though, I have to go. I have so much to finish before morning."

"Okay, I have to call Elliott anyways. Seriously, though, if you want to come and stay with me, just come. No need to call."

"Okay, night."

Hanging up the phone, I looked at the pile of work on my desk, tears stinging my eyes. Why was I having such a hard time with this decision? Blinking, a tear ran down my right cheek. Wiping it away, I took a deep breath and settled into the chair. I put the TV on for background noise and worked away on tomorrow's assignments, taking small bites of my cold dinner.

Chapter Twenty-Four

Tatum

FRIDAY NIGHT HAD FINALLY COME, ONE WEEK DOWN, and only one more to go. Jen was meeting me at the hotel at six. A night of pizza and girl movies was just what I needed.

I pulled into the hotel parking lot, passed my keys to the valet, and headed up to my room. Parker had called the other night while I was asleep, but he hadn't left a message. I had tried calling a couple of times during the day, but he never answered. I was missing him something terrible.

I couldn't wait to relax, so I removed my makeup and changed into a T-shirt and yoga pants. I quickly unpacked my laptop and plugged it in. I had another pile of work that needed to be completed for Monday, and as I looked at all of it, a knock came to the door.

"Your pregnancy test keeper is here with pizza and drinks. Open up," I heard Jen sing from the hallway.

I started to laugh as I made my way to the door. Jen stood there wearing a shit-eating grin.

"Shut up! I don't want the whole building to know," I said, pulling her into the room and shutting the door. I took the pizza from her and placed it on the table.

Jen held out the paper bag between two fingers, rocking it back and forth in front of my face. "Moment of truth?"

"No, let's eat first. I am starving," I said, sitting down on the couch and turning the TV on. "What did you want to watch?"

Jen stood there looking at me, not saying a word.

"What?"

"Nothing, let's eat." Jen sat down on the floor across from me and opened the pizza box while I flipped through the pay-per-view movies. I was trying to avoid the subject while praying that the test would be negative.

It was almost eleven by the time the movie was over, and the pizza was gone. "All right, miss, you have avoided this long enough," she said, rolling over and handing me the bag.

I could feel my stomach flip as I took the bag from her hand. "What if..?" I choked, tears forming in my eyes.

"Well, I guess you'll have to stop burying yourself in denial and actually adult up, go home, and talk to him. Accept the fact about what you want and go for it."

I looked down at the bag in my hand, fear building

inside of me. I looked back up to Jen, my hands starting to shake.

"Listen, we'll cross that bridge when and if we get to it." She looked at me and rubbed my hand.

I walked into the bathroom and shut the door behind me. Taking a deep breath, I opened the bag and removed the test. I stared at the box, my hands starting to shake as I opened it. I fought back nausea as I read and re-read the instructions. Tears were clouding my vision until I could barely see. "Please don't let this be," I whispered to myself. I took the test and put the cap back on it and waited.

"Everything okay?" I heard Jen ask from outside the door.

"Yeah." I pulled the door open and walked out of the bathroom. "We have to wait three minutes before the result. You couldn't have gotten an instant one?" I asked, flopping onto the bed and running my hands over my face. "Is this your form of torture?"

"Oh relax. I'm sure you're most likely just stressed. We are just ruling this out," she said, grinning at me.

I buried my face under my arms and took a deep breath. "I miss him, Jen."

"You haven't heard from him yet?"

"No, he called the other night while I was sleeping, but he didn't leave a message, and he didn't answer when I tried calling him back. What if he never returns my calls again?" I began to cry.

"I'm sure he will. I mean, he has been waiting for you for all these years."

"My God, stop. You sound like Elliott. Now I know you have been hanging around him too long."

"I have not. It's the truth, Tatum."

Rolling my eyes, I got up from the bed and walked into the bathroom. Looking down at the test on the counter, I couldn't believe what I was seeing. I wiped at both eyes and looked again. A lump formed in my throat and tears burned my eyes. There in the little window sat two pink, perfect little lines.

"Did you hear what I said?" I heard Jen ask from behind me, but I didn't answer. I just kept staring down at the counter. "Tatum? What is it?"

I pointed to the test. "It's... It's got to be wrong," I said, holding it up so she could see it. Her eyes left my face and went down to my hands. "Right? It's got to be wrong, right?" The panic built in me the longer she didn't answer. "Jen, say something?"

"I don't know what to say, Tatum. Maybe it's faulty." She picked it up and looked at it. "I can run down to the store and grab another. Don't panic. I'll be right back"

Jen was back in ten minutes. I still hadn't moved from my spot, still staring at that little window in my hand. I took the second test, this one a rapid response so I didn't need to wait, and again, the result was positive.

"You and your damn ideas." I flopped down on the bed and broke into a full-on cry. Jen came over and sat at the end of the bed.

"It's going to be okay, you know," she spoke quietly, smoothing my hair.

"Oh, Jen, what am I going to do?" I sobbed.

"Well, first you need to tell Parker."

"I was afraid you were going to say that. Please, whatever you do, don't tell Elliott. I want Parker to hear it from me, not him."

"You have my word."

I TOOK A BREAK FROM THE PAPERWORK THAT NEEDED TO be finished for Monday morning and decided to watch TV. There was never anything on Sunday nights, and I flipped through the channels trying to find anything that would take my mind off everything.

I picked up my cell and, with a deep breath, dialed Parker. Again, it went straight to voicemail. *He must be working or ignoring me.* I hung up as soon as the machine came on. Why was I being such a coward?

Another deep breath, another dial, and again my call went straight to voice mail. This time, I decided to leave a message. "Hey, it's me. Can you please call me as soon as you get my message? We need to talk." I exhaled as soon as I put the phone down. Who would have thought that would have been such a hard call to make?

Shutting the TV off, I grabbed my phone and laptop and climbed into bed and continued working while I waited for his call.

Chapter Twenty-Five

Parker

Monday afternoon, on my way to work, I checked my voice mail. I had been working a ton of overtime, which was a good thing because as soon as I sat still, my thoughts went to Tatum. At this point, anything to keep her out of my mind was a good thing. It hadn't been one of my smartest moves, to run out on her without giving her a chance to explain, but I was so hurt at the thought of losing her again, I didn't have a choice—my flight response had won. But now all I wanted to do was hear her sexy, sweet voice.

I had decided to shut my phone off last night, so I could get my paperwork caught up before leaving the station. I was even more frustrated with myself when I turned my phone on and found I had missed a call from her. She had called me a few times throughout the week, and I had wanted to return those calls, but by the time work was finished, it was way too late. But last night was the first night she had finally left a message, and she sounded stressed.

I pulled into the parking lot at work and saw my phone flashing with an incoming call from the station.

"Harrison."

"Hey, Parker, it's Randy. I was going over some releases and thought you'd be very interested to know that the guy who assaulted Tatum is out."

"What? When?"

"He was released Thursday. Paperwork states he's to return to his city of residence until his pending court date."

"Fuck, she was supposed to be notified right away. It's Tuesday. He's out for five days without a word. Has anyone spoken with Tatum about this?" I needed to know that she was safe.

"All it says is that a message was left for her regarding this matter."

My heart was in my throat. "All right, thanks. I'm coming into work. I'll stop by in a bit. Thanks, Randy."

Hanging up, I dialed her number. I needed to talk to her before I started work. Her phone rang and rang before going to voicemail. I was worried that if the courts hadn't called her cell phone then the message was sitting on her home machine, which meant she didn't know.

I dialed her number again and held my breath, waiting for her to pick up. Again, it just rang and went to voice mail. I smashed my fist on the steering wheel. I wanted to hear her voice before I went to work, but it looked as if that wasn't going to happen. I sat there for a couple of seconds trying to figure out how to get a hold of her. I didn't know the number to her office, so I did the next best thing and called Elliott.

"Bancroft," I heard Elliott's voice come over the phone.

"Hey, bro. Have you heard from your sister lately?"

"No, why?"

"I just spoke to Randy from the courts. That fucker got released Thursday. I'm wondering if they called her cell or if they just left a message on her home phone. I've been trying to call her, but there is no answer."

"No. She hasn't spoken to me since the night before she left. I admit I was pretty hard on her. But I just got off the phone with Jen, and she said she spent Friday night with her."

"Do you think you can call her back and have her get a hold of Tatum? Or try and call yourself? I want to make sure she knows that he is out. I'll call and leave a message, but please try and call. I want to make sure she is safe. Plus, I have to finish this warrant tonight or else our case is going to shit."

"Yeah, I can."

"Hey, how about after my shift we head up there in the morning? I should be done by six. I'll head home and sleep for a couple hours, and then I'll swing by and pick you up. Say around noon? I'm really missing my girl."

"I think that is a great idea. I'll see you then."

"You got it. I gotta run." Hanging up, I dialed her cell

number again. I didn't want to scare her, but at the same time I wanted her to be aware he had been released.

"You've reached Tatum. Leave me a message."

Tapping my hand on the steering wheel, I heard the beep. "Tatum, baby, it's me. I got your message. I want to talk to you, too, sweetie. I miss you, and I'm sorry for the way I handled things. We can talk tomorrow. I've talked to Elliott; we will be on our way there in the morning.

"I'm not sure if anyone has contacted you or not, but you need to know that Dean has been released. He made bail. He was released on Thursday and he was supposed to be making his way back to the city, Tatum. I hope you get this message soon. Please be safe. I love you."

Hanging up, I took a breath and placed my head against the steering wheel. I hoped to hell this guy wasn't as unhinged as he seemed. If something happened to her, I would never forgive myself.

Chapter Twenty-Six

Dean

IT WAS EARLY AFTERNOON BY THE TIME THE CAR PULLED up outside the Marriott. "You wait, parked around the corner. No matter how long I am, you don't leave, you understand me?"

Getting out of the car, I walked into the hotel and headed to the front desk. "Can I help you, sir?" the clerk behind the counter asked.

"Yes, you can. A friend of mine is staying at this hotel, and I was wondering if you could please tell me what room she is staying in?" I flashed a smile.

"I'm sorry, sir. Unfortunately, policy states that we are unable to give out that kind of information."

"You can't?"

"No, sir." I watched as the woman left the desk and

headed into an adjoining office. I went and took a seat in the lobby. I needed the information.

I had been waiting for about an hour when I took notice of a pretty young girl standing behind the counter. She should be easy to con into giving me the information I required. I waited behind the gentleman she was dealing with. I could tell she was getting flustered with him. When he finally walked away in a huff, she greeted me. "Sir, may I help you?"

"Having a rough day?"

"You could say that."

"I'm sorry to hear. I can't believe that guy would yell at a pretty little thing like you." She blushed and gave a small smile.

"I'm not sure if you can help me. My sister is staying here, and we have had an emergency in the family. I unfortunately don't know the room number she is staying in, but I really need to get a hold of her. Are you able to help me out, sweetheart?"

"I'm sorry, sir," she whispered. "I unfortunately cannot help you. I can't give out that kind of information."

Please, I know you would be breaking the rules, but our father passed away today." A fake tear escaped my eye.

I watched as the young desk clerk glanced over her shoulder at the office behind her. "Well, I'm not supposed to, but I guess I could help you out. What is her name, please?"

"Tatum Bancroft."

She typed her name into the computer and looked up

at me. "Miss. Bancroft is staying in room four-twelve." She gave me a somber look.

"Thank you. I truly appreciate it."

I walked away from the desk and headed up to the fourth floor. I knocked on four-twelve and waited—no answer. I turned and went back to the lobby, sitting off in a far corner to wait until I saw her come in. She was mine, and I wasn't leaving until I taught her the lesson she deserved.

Chapter Twenty-Seven

Tatum

THE SNOW HAD STARTED TO FALL AS I DROPPED MY CAR off to the valet and headed into the hotel. It was almost five and I had been on the go since six this morning. I was tired and hungry, and I just wanted to lounge in front of the TV. I had typed up my resignation and had saved it on my laptop last night before I went to bed. I didn't know how much more of this I could take. I was exhausted and thought about emailing Keller before I left today. Pulling my laptop behind me through the lobby, I stopped at the front desk to place an order for room service. All I wanted was hot tea and chicken soup.

Once I opened the door to my room and turned on the lights, I kicked my shoes off and let my aching feet dig into the thick carpet. I left my bag by the desk and sat down on the edge of the bed, trying to relax. I turned the TV on and headed into the bathroom and started the shower.

Once undressed, I climbed in and let the hot water run over my body; my muscles ached. I stood in the shower and placed my hands on my abdomen, still not believing what those tests had read on Friday night. I had made an appointment with a doctor for next week, once I was back home. I was trying hard not to worry about it until I had confirmation from the doctor, but it wasn't working. Part of me was still worried about what Parker would say when I told him.

Wrapping myself in the plush bathrobe, I glanced at myself in the mirror. Dark circles under my eyes told me I needed way more rest than what I had been getting. I ran a brush through my wet hair and headed back out into the room, noting that room service must have come when I was in the shower because my soup was on the table when I came out.

After I ate, I sat back with my tea and checked my phone for any messages for the first time today. I had worked until almost one in the morning, and I had just enough energy to get to work, never mind bother with anything else.

I had twenty missed calls and three voice mails. Frowning, I searched through the missed calls—a bunch from Parker, one from my brother, and three from Jen. I typed my code in and listened to the first message.

My pulse raced at the sound of Parker's voice. I missed him so much, and then the panic set in. Dean had been released and was on his way back here. He didn't think I would have anything to worry about, but I knew better. If he was out, and he knew I was back here, I would be paid a visit. I hadn't wanted to believe what Elliott had said on the phone the other night, but I knew he was right. It wasn't as if Dean had just become this controlling. He had always been this way; he'd just gotten worse over time. Elliott was right. For all I knew, he was here now, waiting and biding his time before he came to visit.

Getting up and getting dressed, I gathered my stuff from around the room, throwing it into my bag. I had to get out of here, and Jen was the closest. Parker wouldn't be here until at least eight tonight, and that was if he was on time. I couldn't risk waiting. I called Jen as I ran around grabbing more of my things.

"Hey, Tatum! I was going to call you. The guys are on their way here."

"Jen, Dean is on his way back to the city." I started to cry. "I have to get out of here."

"Tatum, calm down."

"No, you don't understand, I can't calm down. If he knows where I am, he will come here."

"Okay, I'm coming to get you."

"There isn't time. I will be there in twenty minutes."

"Okay, I'll be waiting. I'll call Elliott and Parker and let them know to come here. If anything goes wrong, call me."

I was having a hard time catching my breath as I stuffed the last few things I would need into my bag and snapped it shut.

"And, Tatum, calm down before you get in the car and drive please."

"See you soon." I hung up the phone and grabbed my charger out of the wall and threw it along with my phone into my purse.

I shut off the TV, threw my shoes on, and grabbed my purse and bag and pulled the door open. Taking a step around the corner, I felt myself being roughly pushed back into the room, a chest in my face.

"Well, here you are. You all alone? Or is he here?" Dean asked, looking around the room before shutting the door behind him and locking the deadbolt.

I stepped back away from him. "I'm alone. What do you want?"

He glanced to the bags in my hand. "Are you going somewhere?"

I shook my head, trying to remain calm.

"Cause it certainly looks like you were planning on leaving in a hurry. We need to have a little talk." He took a couple of steps, closing the distance between us. "Seems to me, not too long ago, you accused me of cheating on you. Now I hear you are fucking that cop. What's that all about, Tatum?"

I studied him, noticing the vein protruding in his neck. "No." I swallowed hard. "I'm not sleeping with anyone," I lied, dropping my bags to the floor.

"I'm going to give you another chance. You know how I feel about liars. So, are you sure about that?" He squinted, taking me in.

I was paralyzed with fear, unable to answer him.

"Well?" He took a quick step forward and wrapped his fist around my throat, cracking my head into the wall as he threw me against it. Pain shot through the back of my head, and it took me a couple of seconds to regain my bearings.

"Answer me, and don't fucking lie!" he yelled, clenching his teeth together. "After I paid you a visit last time, he had me put in jail for trying to fuck my own girl. Do you know what that will do to my career?" He gripped my throat tighter, cutting off more air.

I grabbed at his hands and tried to pry them away from my throat.

"What's the problem? Can't breathe?" He laughed.

Tears were burning my eyes. He released his hold enough for me to take in a breath. I was still clawing at his hands to let me go when he grabbed my arms with his free hand and held them together.

"You think I don't know? That's cute." He leaned in closer and whispered in my ear, "Fucking him on your back deck, Tatum, really? Nothing should surprise me with a whore like you. Your behavior is disgusting. What do you have to say for yourself?"

I started to squirm and fight back tears while trying to breathe, the tightness in my chest unbelievable. Finally, he let go of my throat and turned away from me.

"I didn't, I swear to you. He's just a friend," I cried as I tried my best to catch my breath, rubbing at my throat.

He laughed. "Listen to you. You sound pathetic. I didn't, I swear. He's just a friend," he mimicked. "What the fuck are you doing with that guy, Tatum?"

"I swear to you, nothing is going on." I never saw it

coming. He turned and smashed his fist into my face, knocking me to the floor.

"You fucked him!" he screamed over me, clenching his fists.

Rage spilled through him as he bent down and pulled me up by the arms. A fist to the other side of my face sent pain searing through my head as he dropped me back to the ground. I let out a sob, my head throbbing. I could taste blood.

"Get up!" he screamed.

I lay there, unable to move, my head ringing.

"I told you to get. The. Fuck. Up!"

"I'm sorry," I sobbed.

He grabbed me by both arms and held me up against the wall. "You're what? You're sorry?" A laugh emanated from his chest. "Sorry doesn't even begin to cut it, you bitch." Gripping me by the throat again, I struggled to breath. "I told you, you were mine, but you didn't want to bother with me. Instead, you ran away, and right to that pussy. I'm not even sure I want your filthy ass now, but I'll be dammed if I leave you for him."

He let go of me, holding me against the wall with his body. With his hand gripping my chin, he lifted my head. "Look at me."

I struggled to open my eyes. My cheeks were swelling, and the light in the room was making it hard to open them.

"Open. Your. Fucking. Eyes," he demanded.

The last thing I felt was his hand connect with my face, before I fell to the floor.

Chapter Twenty-Eight

Parker

ELLIOTT AND I WERE ABOUT AN HOUR AWAY YET. WE
had pulled over to get gas and switch seats. I had driven
most of the way, but I was exhausted after working all
night with only a couple hours sleep. We had just gotten
back onto the highway when Elliott's phone rang.

"Bancroft," Elliott answered.

"Elliott, it's me. Tatum was supposed to be here over an
hour ago. She hasn't shown up yet. She called me after she
got Parker's message. She was pretty panicked."

"Did you try calling her?" Elliott asked.

"I have. There was no answer."

I felt panic rise in me.

"Jen, are you okay to go over to the place she is staying?" Elliott asked.

"Yep."

"All right, we are still about forty-five minutes away. We'll be there as soon as we can be. Call us back once you get there."

"Sure thing, Elliott."

Elliott hung up his phone as I sat staring down at mine waiting for a response to the text I'd sent her. A bad feeling hit my gut.

"It'll be okay, Parker."

"Do you think you can drive faster, Elliott?" I asked. Staring down at my phone, I felt the truck speed up. The last time I had rushed to her side was back in college, and I had the same sick feeling in my stomach now as I did then.

"I can't make the game tonight, Parker. I have to head back to my dorm and study. Plus, Mom and Dad are going to be calling me before we head out to the party," Tatum said as she loaded her books into her bag.

"Okay, sweets. I will text you as soon as the game is over. Then I will come and get you," I said, placing a kiss on her lips. I brushed a strand of hair from her face as I looked deep into her eyes and leaned in for another kiss.

I sent a text to Tatum as soon as I hit the changing room. I decided to shower there instead of going back to my dorm room. I had to pick her up in an hour anyway. After my shower, I checked my phone. There was nothing yet, so I took my equipment and headed to my car.

After loading everything into my trunk, I sat down behind the wheel and pulled my phone from my pocket. It had been forty-five minutes; this was odd for her. I dialed her number. Again, nothing.

A sick feeling came over me. Something was wrong. I started my car and popped it into reverse and headed over to her dorm.

I walked down the hall to her dorm room, people giving me strange looks and whispering to one another. Frowning, I stood outside her door. I went to knock when I heard a deep, strangled sob from the other side.

"Tatum?" I called, my heart in my throat.

The door opened, and Tatum stood on the other side facing me, tears running down her beautiful face.

"What is it, baby?"

She ran into my arms, crying into my chest. I held her for a while, until I noticed a bunch of eyes on us. I walked into her room and shut the door behind me, so we could have some privacy.

"What's going on, baby?"

"It's my parents. There was an accident."

"I can take you home tonight. Does Elliott know?"

She was freezing as I rubbed her arms, trying to calm her down. She nodded her head.

"They're dead."

The words rang through my head, the emptiness in her eyes scaring me. Grabbing hold of her, I pulled her against me and wrapped her in my arms. As she cried against me, I wished at that moment I could take every ounce of pain she was feeling away from her.

I picked her up and carried her over to her bed. I placed her down on the mattress, kicked my shoes off, crawled in behind her, and pulled her against me, holding her as tight as I could. I wanted to let her know I would never let her go.

A phone rang, bringing me out of my memory. I

glanced down to the screen on my phone and saw there was still no response.

"Hey, Jen," Elliott answered.

"Elliott, I'm at the Marriott. I walked in and almost ran into Dean. He was leaving the elevator as I came in. He had blood splattered across his white T-shirt, Elliott. I ducked out of sight, praying he didn't see me. He went out front and climbed into a black Audi that was waiting at the side of the road."

We looked at one another when we both realized what Jen had said. That was the same color and make of car that had been following Tatum.

"Is Tatum okay?"

"Honestly, I don't know, Elliott. I called you as soon as I saw him."

"Were you able to get a plate, Jen?" I asked.

"I got a partial plate. I called the police, Parker."

"Jen, get hotel security to go up to the room with you," Elliott suggested. "We should be there in about twenty minutes." Elliott hung up and sped up.

"Man, I can't take this, Elliott. I hope to God she is okay. I'll never forgive myself if anything happens to her."

Elliott was quiet as he concentrated on the road. I kept dialing her number to keep my mind occupied. I couldn't take it anymore. The phone rang and rang, and I sat there praying that she would answer. Hanging up to dial again, the phone rang once and suddenly she answered. A faint voice was all I heard on the other end.

"Help me."

"Tatum?"

Again, the same faint voice came over the phone. "Parker. Help me."

I could hear my heart beating in my ears. "I'm almost there. Hang on, baby." I looked at Elliott and saw relief wash over his face as he sped up more. I finally heard Jen's voice in the background with paramedics and police.

"Parker, it's me," Jen's voice came over the phone. "They are taking her to Johnson's Memorial over on Fifth Avenue," Jen said.

Relief washed over me that they had gotten to her. "We're on our way. Meet you there."

Chapter Twenty-Nine

Parker

WE HAD FINALLY ARRIVED AND PARKED IN THE emergency parking. Elliott and I rushed into the hospital's emergency entrance. Looking around, we spotted Jen over in the corner, her head in her phone.

"How is she?" Elliott and I called over to her at the same time.

Jen looked up with tears in her eyes and got up out of her seat. "I shouldn't have waited so long. I didn't get there in time. He got to her first." Her lips trembled. "He was covered in blood, and then I found her."

Elliott took her in his arms. She was in shock.

"I'm so sorry to the both of you," she said through broken sobs.

Elliott pulled her into him and comforted her. "Where is she, Jen?"

"She was taken for x-rays to make sure nothing has been broken. She may need stitches. She was barely conscious when I found her." She buried her head in Elliott's chest and continued crying.

I could feel the anger pulse through my veins. "Fucker!" I began pacing back and forth. "If I get my hands on him, I'll kill him. I should have killed him when I had the fucking chance."

"Parker, relax, man. The cops have been notified. I'm sure they are on their way to pick him up."

"Doesn't matter. He's a piece of shit, and you know how I feel about these pieces of shit, Elliott. This is different now. This is personal."

"Yes, Parker, I do. He is a piece of shit, but he isn't worth your anger. It's more important that we deal with Tatum. She is going to need our help. She is going to need you."

I ran my hand through my hair and sat down on one of the chairs, trying to calm myself down. Elliott was right; I needed to focus my energy on her, on us.

"I'm sorry. I feel like I have let you both down. I should have just gone and picked her up when she first called," Jen said through broken sobs.

I looked at her and smiled. "All that matters, is you found her and she is okay." I reached out and rubbed her shoulder. "How about we grab some coffee while we wait?" I nodded to the machine in the corner.

We sat down in the waiting area and sipped our coffees.

I hated waiting. I never was very patient man when it came to shit like this. I was about to refill my cup when a set of double doors opened and a doctor approached us.

"Are you folks with Tatum Bancroft?"

Jen stood. "Yes, I'm Jennifer, her best friend, Elliott, her brother, and Parker, her boyfriend."

"Elliott, may I speak to you in private please?"

Elliott stood up and took a step forward, grabbing Jen's hand. "Doctor, please, these people are family to me and to Tatum. Whatever you have to say, you can say it to all of us."

He nodded at Elliott. "Okay. I have her resting. We have given her what we can for pain, taking her condition into consideration. I was concerned about the trauma to her jaw, so we took some x-rays. Nothing is broken. I'm confident that she is going to be fine."

I stared at him. "What do you mean when you say considering her condition?"

"Her blood work shows that she is pregnant. From the results, it looks like she is about one or two months along. We will do an ultrasound in a couple of days to confirm how far along she is and to make sure everything is okay."

I couldn't believe my ears. "She's what?"

Elliott patted me on the shoulder. "It's okay, Parker. I think you're in shock." He smiled to the doctor and Jen.

"Does she know?"

"She knew, and she is very worried about the baby, so I want no added stress on her other than what she already has," he said, looking at us for the next round of questions.

"When can we see her?" Jen asked, reaching for my hand and giving it a squeeze.

"I would like her to rest as much as she can before we move her up to a room, but I can't see any reason that you can't see her. I want you to go one at a time and not for very long, okay? She needs her rest tonight. Whenever you're ready, head through these door around the corner to the right. She is in room eight."

"When do you think she can be released?"

"Well, we want to make sure the fetus is okay and that she doesn't have a concussion, so a couple of days. She will need to stay with someone for about two weeks, once she is released. Are there any more questions I can answer for you at this time?"

We looked to one another and shook our heads no.

"Well, then I shall get back to my rounds. I will see you tomorrow." He nodded to us and went back through the same double doors he had come out of.

I sat down, completely shocked. I was going to be a father. I looked up at Elliott who stood watching me. "I hope you're not going to kill me, man." He gave me a smile. "I swear to you we were careful, but I assure you I will look after her," I said, holding my hands up.

Elliott chuckled to himself. "No, man. I'm just glad it's you. There has never been a time that I can remember when I wasn't okay with you being in her life." He patted me on the back and reached out and pulled Jen into him.

"When you're ready, why don't you go see her tonight? Jen and I are going to call the police department, see if they need anything else answered."

I nodded. It was going to take all the strength in the world I had to restrain myself from walking out those doors after seeing her, because I knew I would want to hunt him down and kill him. I just hoped that I was strong enough to hold myself together.

I took a deep breath and exhaled. I watched Elliott and Jen walk over to a dark corner and sit down together, Elliott making the phone call while Jen rested her head on his shoulder. I took another deep breath and stood, walking toward the double doors, toward my girl.

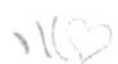

I OPENED THE DOOR AND PEEKED AROUND THE CORNER. Two nurses sat at the desk filling out paperwork. They paid no attention to me as I walked into room eight. The room was dark, and Tatum was sound asleep, the sound of her monitors creating a soothing rhythm. I watched the slow rise and fall of her chest from the doorway. She looked so helpless lying in that bed.

It wasn't until I got closer to her that I noticed the dark bruises on her face and a large gash across her eyebrow and cheek. Both had been stitched closed. There was bruising on her neck and arms, too. A nurse walked in to check her vitals and added something into her IV bag.

"You guys took photographs of all her injuries, correct?" I couldn't help the cop coming out in me, but they would be needed for evidence should this bastard try to get off.

"Yes, sir. The police were here and took down everything." She continued adjusting wires, and then went back out to the desk.

I looked down at Tatum, tears threatening to roll down my cheeks at any moment. I could feel the rage growing inside of me, the anger I carried for not being there for her, to protect her.

"I'm so sorry, baby girl. I'm sorry I wasn't there to protect you from him. I'm sorry I was so angry with you. Never again," I whispered to her, leaning down and placing a soft kiss on her forehead.

I took her hand in mine and sat down in the chair beside her bed. At my touch, she stirred, and I heard her mumble my name.

"I'm here, baby, right here. I'm not going anywhere."

She slowly opened her eyes and looked at me. "Parker, what are you doing here? I don't want you to see me like this." A single tear ran over her cheek as she tried to turn away from me, a grimace coming over her face as the pain caught her.

"See you like what? You're my girl. No different than when I saw you a week ago." I smiled, trying to keep my tears at bay.

"I look awful."

"You're beautiful." She grew quiet as we stared into each other's eyes. "You're still the same woman I fell in love with." I smiled at her and gently wiped the tears from her cheek.

"Did they catch him?" she asked, looking up at me with tired eyes.

"I'm not sure yet, baby. Elliott is outside with Jen. They

were calling to find out. We will make sure that once he is caught he stays locked away."

"Elliott's here as well?" She closed her eyes as a small sob came from her throat. "Does he know everything?"

"Yes, but you don't need to worry about anything. You just need to concentrate on healing and getting stronger so that..." I rested my hand on her abdomen and squeezed her hand with my other.

She closed her eyes. "They told you?" she asked in a barely audible whisper.

"They did." I smiled down at her.

"I was afraid that they would tell you."

"Why would you be afraid of that?" What came next almost knocked me to my knees and took my breath away.

"I wanted to be the one to tell you. I wasn't sure you would want it. I wasn't sure you would even want to be with me after everything that happened."

I felt the air being sucked from the room. My heart ached for this beautiful woman who lay before me. I had wanted her for years, and I had never given up hope that she would find her way back to me. She owned my heart and would until the day I ceased to exist.

I rested myself on my opposite arm and bent down to place a long, gentle kiss on her mouth. "I've always wanted you. Always. even after you walked away from me the first time." I kissed her again. "Close your eyes, baby, and get some rest."

I sat down in the chair beside her and held her hand, watching as she closed her eyes. It wasn't long before she fell into a sound sleep.

TATUM

WE HAD TALKED EXTENSIVELY OVER THE COUPLE OF DAYS that he stayed by my side in the hospital. Talked right into the wee hours of the morning both nights. Things turned serious when we started talking about the baby.

Parker leaned back against the chair he was sitting in, his feet up on the bed. I could see he had the weight of the world on his shoulders at that moment. I hadn't seen that look on his face since the day we went our separate ways.

"What is it?" I asked quietly.

"What?"

"You look like you have something on your mind. Talk to me." I raised the bed up a little higher.

"It's nothing."

"I don't think it's nothing. Talk to me."

I watched as Parker swallowed and turned his eyes down to the floor. "I'm still a little shocked. We're going to have a baby together."

"Yes. But I gave it some thought last night. If you don't want to be involved, then just say the words."

I couldn't help it. I was nervous. I was pissed that the doctor had told him. I didn't want him to feel obligated to stay with me. I couldn't seem to get it through my head that someone would want to be with me after everything that had happened.

"I'm not him, Tatum."

My head snapped up, and I locked eyes with him.

"I'm not him. Stop doubting what we have. I can see it written all over your face. I'm in love with you, no matter what you have been through. I'm here, and this time I am not going anywhere, no matter how long it takes you to realize it."

I felt a tear slip down my cheek. "Why did I ever let you go?" I covered my eyes with my hands. I didn't want him to see me cry again. I had shed enough tears in the last week.

"Move in with me?"

I slowly lowered my hands and looked at him. I studied the look on his face and could tell he was serious. He stood up from the chair and sat down beside me in the bed and took both of my hands into his, his warm touch sending a pulse through my body.

"Move in with me?" His deep voice soothed my nerves almost instantly.

"What about my place?"

"We can worry about that later. What do you say?"

It took me a few minutes, but then I heard Jen's words in my head. *You'll have to stop burying yourself in denial. You just need the guts to admit it to yourself.*

I nodded my head. "Yes."

He pushed me back against the pillow and kissed me deeply, the heat from his body soothing me. At that moment, a feeling of comfort came over me, as if my soul knew I was home.

Parker stayed for a while, and we watched a couple of shows together. He was just starting to nod off when I shook him.

"What is it?"

"Listen, you're exhausted. Why don't you go spend the night with Jen and Elliott? We have a long day tomorrow."

"No, no, I am fine," he said, standing up to stretch.

"Seriously, babe, go. Get a good night's rest."

He looked from me to the bench he had been sleeping on and back to me.

"It's okay. I'm good."

I forced Parker to leave shortly after making sure I had everything I needed for the night. Parker hadn't left my side since I was admitted. He had slept in the chair in Emergency for the first night, and the last two nights on that horrible, hard bench in my room. He was exhausted and needed a good night's sleep before we headed home tomorrow. I couldn't wait to get out of here and on with my life.

Chapter Thirty

Tatum

WE HAD BEEN HOME FOR ABOUT A WEEK NOW. IT HAD been strange at first living here, but I was settling in. Parker had brought over a bunch of my clothing from my place, and I had just finished putting it away. We would go over tomorrow to get a few of my other things. I was glad he had asked me to move in with him. The other place held one nasty memory I couldn't seem to forget when I was there alone. I didn't tell him that, but I think deep down he knew. We had decided to rent out my place, and we wanted to get it cleaned out and rented as soon as possible.

It was a little after ten when I sat down with a cup of tea to read the newspaper. I was waiting for Parker to get home from work when my phone rang.

"How are you feeling?" Elliott's voice came over the phone.

"Doing okay." I smiled. "What about you?"

"Good. Jen and I should be leaving tomorrow. Looks like everything is all ready. We will call you guys once we arrive."

"Great! I can't wait to see you both."

"I can't wait to see you either."

"Elliott, I wanted to say I am sorry, and I am grateful for you." I felt he had to hear it; he had to know.

I heard the front door open and glanced around the corner to see Parker taking off his shoes. He looked so hot in his uniform.

"Listen, Parker just got home. See you tomorrow?"

"You got it. Oh, and the same goes for me." I heard him swallow hard then heard Jen yell bye in the background before I hung up.

Smiling to myself, I got up off the couch and walked into the kitchen. Parker looked beat.

"Hey, beautiful!" Wrapping me in his arms, he kissed me gently. "How was your day?"

"It was good. Yours?"

"Don't ask!" he said, kissing me again. "Who were you talking to?"

"Elliott. They will be back in town tomorrow. They called to let us know," I said, leaning into him.

"How was your doctor's appointment today? I wanted to go with you, but I couldn't even get a minute to call you."

"Everything is good. The baby is going to be fine."

"I can't even begin to tell you how happy I am to hear that." He leaned in for another kiss. "I'm going to go and have a shower."

"Did you want anything to eat?"

"No. I ate dinner late. How about tea?"

I nodded as he headed to the bathroom. Parker was still in the shower when I brought the tea into the living room. I lay down on the oversized couch and pulled the blanket over me then turned on the TV. Once I had found a movie to watch, I relaxed back into the cushions and shut all the lights off. It wasn't long before I drifted off.

I jumped a little when I felt the couch sink down, and I opened my eyes.

"It's just you." I smiled and looked into Parker's eyes. He lay down beside me.

"Yep, it's just me. Come here," he whispered as he placed his arm around me and pulled me into him, pulling the blanket up around me.

I rested my head on his chest, breathing in his cologne. It truly felt like home in his arms.

I WOKE UP AND LOOKED AT THE CLOCK. IT WAS ALREADY nine. I crawled out of bed and headed to the kitchen to make some tea. Parker had already left for the day and would be home in time to head over to help Elliott and Jen when they arrived.

I grabbed my phone and checked my email. The only

one that caught my eye was from Brad Keller. I still hadn't let him know about my decision, and he was asking.

I took my tea into the living room and sat down on the couch. Parker and I had talked, and we both decided that work could wait until after the baby was born. Being pregnant, he didn't want me to travel back and forth. I took another sip of my tea and dialed Brad's number.

"Brad speaking."

"Hi, Brad, it's Tatum."

"Tatum, how are you feeling? We are very concerned about you."

"I'm doing better, thanks for asking. I got your email this morning, and I wanted to call you back."

"Well, I am glad that you did. Listen, there is no rush. I know that you are on medical leave, but I wanted to know how long it will be before we can expect you back?"

"Thank you. I am happy that you are so understanding. But considering all that has happened, I have decided that I will not be returning. I wanted to thank you, though, for the opportunity."

"Is it the travel that you are concerned about? We have been thinking about that. We really want you to stay with us. That is why I went to the president and talked to him about you. He is willing to make your position remote. You will be able to work from home and will only be required to come to the office a few times a year."

I went quiet. This was not how I planned this to go. "I thank you for that, but I am going to have to decline. I will be sending in my formal resignation to you once I get to my laptop." I swallowed hard. As much as I loved working, I knew this was the right thing to do.

"I am sorry to hear that, Tatum. I want to wish you all the best."

"Thank you, Brad. I wish you all the best as well." I hung up the phone and sat back against the couch. I didn't feel bad about quitting. I was actually relieved and happy to know I was going to finally start my life with Parker and our son or daughter.

I had spent the rest of the day doing laundry and looking online for some things for the baby's room. We had decided to turn the bedroom across from ours into the nursery, and I wanted to take my time picking things out. I looked up at the clock. Elliott and Jen should arrive any minute.

I was about to start dinner when my phone pinged with a message. I looked down at the phone and saw a message from Jen.

JEN: "ABOUT TWENTY MINUTES AWAY! SEE YOU SOON!"

I smiled at the message and typed out a quick response as Parker walked through the door.

"Hey, beautiful."

"Hey. How was your day?"

"All right. Listen, how about you come and sit down. I have news."

The look on his face told me something was wrong. "What is it?"

"Just come over here and sit down please."

I walked over to the table and took a seat. He sat down beside me and took hold of my hand.

"I got a call today from your lawyer."

A funny feeling started to grow in the pit of my stomach. "Has he been released?" I felt a rush of heat run up my body. "Please don't tell me he has been released. I don't think I can handle that."

"No, he hasn't been released."

I felt the breath I hadn't even known I have been holding leave my body.

"They found him this morning in his cell. Dead."

I stared at Parker, not sure what to say. I wasn't even sure how to feel about this. I was angry that he would not be punished for what he had done to me. But a huge part of me was glad I would never have to see him again.

"What happened? "I choked out the words, barely recognizing my own voice.

"Well, it's still under investigation, but the lawyer said it looks like it may have been either a massive heart attack or a stroke."

I sat there for a minute, taking in what he had said. At that moment, a sense of peace came over me as I looked at Parker, trying to digest this new information. It was over. I would never have to worry about seeing him ever again, whether it be in a court room in a few months or on the street in some city somewhere years from now. I didn't need to worry if I didn't lock a door at night. He simply wasn't coming back. That knowledge was probably the best present I could have asked for.

"Are you okay, Tatum?"

As he asked me that, a flood of emotion ran through my body, and all the tension and stress I had been carrying the last few months released itself. "I'm good."

I stood from my chair and straddled his lap. As he wrapped his strong arms around me, I nuzzled my face into his neck. "I love you. Thank you."

"Thank you for what?"

"For coming back into my life when you did, and for showing me my way home to you." My lips met his, and I kissed him deeply.

Epilogue

Tatum - *19 months later*

I T WAS C HRISTMAS E VE, AND THE SPARKLING TREE IN the corner of the darkened living room gave off the smell of fresh pine. I had always loved the smell of a fresh tree. I had put Emma down for the night and had just finished wrapping the last of my gifts for Parker. I had my chamomile tea, and I curled up under the blanket on the couch and threw on some soft Christmas music. I looked out the window at the falling snow; it was so beautiful.

Hearing a key in the door, I smiled to myself. I had missed him something terrible today. I listened as I heard him throw his keys on the counter and drop his duffel bag on the floor then the familiar sound of his footsteps as he walked into the room.

"There's my girl!"

The sound of his voice sent a chill through my body.

He came up behind me and kissed my neck, his breath ticking as he asked, "How was your day?"

I smiled as he wrapped his arms around me from behind. "It was good. Jen and I went out to shop. You should have seen Emma; she was so mesmerized by all the lights." I smiled, thinking of her little smile. "What about your day?"

"You don't even want to know. Christmas always brings out the best in people. Is Emma asleep?" I nodded. "I'm going to peek in on her then get showered."

He met my lips for another kiss. "Did you want tea?"

"Please, I won't be long."

I gave a soft smile. "Go see your daughter." I could always tell when he had had a particularly rough day because he always went in to see her after his shift. He never woke her; he would just stare down at her little sleeping body.

I shut off the TV and unplugged the tree and headed into the kitchen to make our tea. Carrying both mugs into the bedroom, I turned the bedside lights on and pulled the curtains. It was cold; the snow was falling harder than before, and it was piling up fast. I flipped on the gas fireplace and crawled into bed. It had been a long day, and I was tired.

I was lying in bed with my eyes closed when I heard Parker come in. "Emma still asleep?" I asked, watching Parker walk to his side of the bed in nothing but a small, white towel.

"Yep, out like a light. Sorry I took so long. I could stare

at her forever, she is just so perfect," he said, crawling toward me looking me in the eyes. "Just like you." His expression grew serious as he wrapped his arms around me, leaned down, and kissed me under my ear and down my neck.

I could melt in his arms, that was how much I loved being held by him. Placing his hand on my cheek, he kissed me slowly and passionately, his tongue finding mine. He pulled me into him as he lay back against the pillow, and I rested my head on his chest.

"What else did you do today?" he asked while rubbing my shoulder.

"I went to the doctor," I whispered.

"What's wrong? Is something wrong with Emma?" Alarm filled his voice.

"No, Emma is fine. Her checkup isn't until after Christmas."

"You not feeling well?" he said, sitting up and leaning on his one arm, looking into my eyes.

"I'll be okay. Nothing that seven or eight months won't fix," I said, giving him a gentle smile.

He looked at me a little confused, and then his eyes lit up. "Are you serious?"

I nodded, tears coming to my eyes. "Are you happy?"

He leaned down and kissed my mouth hard. "Happy? Are you kidding? I am ecstatic." He kissed me again, taking me in his arms. "God, I am so in love with you," he murmured between kisses.

I could feel him grow hard against me as he kissed me harder and deeper. He moved on top of me, and I opened my legs to accommodate him. I could feel him at my entrance, and he slowly slid into me, filling and stretching me. He let out a deep moan as he pushed himself inside of me, all the way to the hilt. I could feel the pressure building inside of me as he gave a few slow, deep strokes. It didn't take long. I could feel myself tightening around him as he swelled and throbbed. A few more deep pumps, and I felt him fill me, and he collapsed on top of me, breathing hard.

Emma started to cry, getting louder by the second.

"I'll get her," he said, pulling out of me and cleaning himself off with his towel.

I lay back and watched him walk out of the bedroom.

Minutes later, he came walking back into the bedroom with a giggling Emma in his arms. "You sure know how to ruin a moment, don't you, princess," he spoke to her in the softest voice, looking down into her face. "I think she is hungry." He held up a bottle in his other hand and laid her down beside me. He crawled into bed, spooning me, and we watched Emma drink her bottle and fall off to sleep.

*P*ARKER

WHEN I WOKE, TATUM AND EMMA WERE BOTH STILL asleep. I went into the kitchen, put some light Christmas music on, and pulled the turkey out of the fridge. Jen and Elliott would be on their way over later this morning to see their goddaughter. I wanted to get as much done and out of the way before they got here as possible.

I went about making my magical stuffing and got the bird ready. I had just slid it in the oven when I heard soft footsteps behind me.

Tatum wrapped her arms around my waist and pressed herself into me. "Merry Christmas."

"Merry Christmas, beautiful." I turned so I could take her in my arms and kiss her. "Would you like some coffee, freshly brewed?"

"Mmm, yes, please. Emma is still asleep."

I leaned over and placed another deep kiss on her lips. "Well, go sit down. I just need to finish up, and I'll be right in."

I took the mugs out of the cupboard. Once I was sure she was out of the kitchen, I took a deep breath and reached inside the pockets of my house pants. I gripped the small box that was hiding there and prayed that this time her answer would be different.

Elliott and Jen had been building up my courage to ask Tatum to marry me. Jen had pretty much guaranteed that she wouldn't turn me down.

I cleaned up the mess that I had made and figured I had stalled enough. I picked up the full mugs and made my way into the living room. Tatum sat curled up on the couch taking in the warmth of the fire while watching the lights blink on the tree. I put the mugs down in front of her and sat down on the edge of the couch beside her.

"What's that?" I nodded in the direction of the tree.

As soon as she turned her head to look, I slipped down

on one knee and took the box out of my pocket and held it in my hand.

"What's what?" she asked, turning to me and taking me in.

"I wanted to do this a long time ago, years, in fact, but things didn't quite go as planned on that day." I swallowed hard, taking her small hand in mine. I got all the reassurance I needed when I felt her squeeze my hand. I held up the ring and immediately her eyes filled with tears. "It was always you, Tatum. It always has been you, and it always will be you. Spend the rest of your life with me? Will you marry me, baby girl?" I almost choked on the words, I was so nervous.

She blinked away the tears, and with her other hand wiped her cheeks. "Yes."

I removed the ring from the box and slid it onto her finger, feeling more complete than I ever had. I pulled her into me and gave her a deep kiss, tasting the saltiness of her tears on her lips. Emma let out a shrill cry from the other room, letting us both know she was awake and ready to start her day. I had everything I had ever wanted right here under this roof.

Note from the Author

Dear Readers, I wanted to thank you for taking the time to read my book. I hope you enjoyed Parker and Tatum's story. If you did, please consider leaving a review on Amazon and Goodreads. Thank you for your support.

Finding Forever with You
(The Malone Brothers Book 4)
Release Date: May 29, 2020

My best friend Sophie was gorgeous, at times uptight and desperate.

Her biological clock was ticking and after yet another failed relationship she pulled me aside.

"Listen Chase, you know I adore you and you know I need you. Historically, you always come through for me." She swallowed hard while I listened. "It's no secret that I want a baby, the semi old fashioned way."

I nodded not really believing what I was hearing.

"I want you to do it."

"You want my swimmers?"

"Yes, through natural injection."

Sex with my best friend. The best friend I had once upon a time wanted in a bad way.

"Don't worry, I've got this covered," I assured her. She looked relieved and maybe even a little excited.

Seven Days, Six nights, and lots of sex. What more could I want?

Oh right. A way to turn this into forever so I could raise my child too.

Preorder

Add to TBR

Vegas MMA

Dagger, the first book in the all new Vegas MMA series is here.

Derrick

I'd been fighting all my life.
Making it my career choice seemed...logical.
Sticking to what I was good at seemed...illogical as often as I ended up in the ER.

Then my occupational hazard began to feel like more of a perk when I met, Katy. She was a night nurse at the ER I frequented. She could barely hide her contempt for me, which naturally made the curvy brunette with long wavy hair all the more irresistible.

Now I just needed to convince her I was a better lover than a fighter.

Katy

They called him Dagger, for the looks he gave.
He knew I hated him on sight, but still, he teased me and tried to sway me.

There's no way it would work. I was on the run and still healing from a relationship with a 'roid-raging powerlifter. No way was I going to give it a go with someone trained to cause pain for a living.

Then my ex tracked me down. And suddenly, having a fighter in my corner didn't seem like such a bad idea.

Read Chapter One Here
Start Reading Today

Add all Vegas MMA Books to your TBR

Dagger
Ace
Blade
Trigger
Wrath
Cain

Other Titles from S.L. Sterling

Standalones
> It Was Always You
> Bad Company
> On A Silent Night
> Back to You this Christmas

THE MALONE BROTHERS
> A Kiss Beneath the Stars (The Malone Brothers 1)
> In Your Arms (The Malone Brothers 2)
> His to Hold (The Malone Brothers 3)

VEGAS MMA
> Dagger

About the Author

S.L. Sterling has been an avid reader since she was a child, often found getting lost in books. Today if she isn't writing, she can be found buried in a romance novel. S.L. Sterling lives with her husband and two dogs in Northern Ontario.

Sign up for my
Newsletter

Visit my
Website

Join my Street Team
Sterlings Silver Sapphires